STARS IN HER EYES

Tom's voice was as warm and rich as Linda remembered it. The words captured exactly what she had been feeling about Shane.

> *Time goes so slowly*
> *You can feel so lost and lonely*
> *Love has its own kind of time.*

But how long do you have to wait? Linda wondered. *How long did it take before you'd know if the love you felt was real—or if it wasn't?* Tom seemed to understand her feelings, at least in his songs. He must have felt the same way once.

Linda felt bad about putting Tom off. But what else could she have done? She loved Shane, and he certainly seemed to care about her. She thought about the other song—the one Shane had written for her. Were those feelings of love he had expressed? If he didn't love her, why would he have written that song?

Bantam Sweet Dreams Romances
Ask your bookseller for the books you have missed

Stars In Her Eyes

Dee Daley

BANTAM BOOKS
TORONTO • NEW YORK • LONDON • SYDNEY • AUCKLAND

STARS IN HER EYES
A Bantam Book / October 1987

ISBN 0-553-26419-2

Published simultaneously in the United States and Canada

Reproduced, printed and bound in Great Britain by
Hazell Watson & Viney Limited,
Member of the BPCC Group,
Aylesbury, Bucks

Stars In Her Eyes

Chapter One

"We will be making our descent into New York's La Guardia Airport in just a few moments." The flight attendant's gentle voice interrupted Linda Wills's thoughts. "The tower reports that the temperature on the ground is a very pleasant seventy-five degrees with clear, sunny skies." As the woman spoke, Linda's ears popped. She knew that meant that they were getting ready to land soon.

She turned and looked out the small window on the right side of the plane as it gently banked to the right over Manhattan. Between the wispy clouds, Linda could see the enormous city below her. She could pick out the spires of the Empire State Building and the Chrysler Building, which reached high into the bright sky.

There was also a rolling patch of green and brown that lay directly below the plane then. *That has to be Central Park*, she thought. The whole city glittered in the bright morning sunshine.

The flight attendant came by and checked to see if Linda's seat belt was fastened properly. The young woman had been friendly during the whole trip, telling Linda about New York and answering her many questions. She smiled now and said, "I hope everything works out for you here. It really is a great city. And if you want to learn about art, this is the place to be."

Linda smiled back. "Thanks. And thanks for filling me in. I really appreciate it."

"You're welcome. I'm glad I could help." Then she headed toward the back of the plane. Linda leaned back in her seat as the plane swung around for its final approach. She thought back to earlier that morning when her mother and father had seen her off at the airport in Kansas City. Linda knew her mother had been crying that morning; she had seen the redness in her familiar pale blue eyes. Her father, on the other hand, had just smiled quietly. That was the great thing about her father, she thought. She could always count on him to reassure her when things were frightening or confusing. And whenever she had a crisis (sometimes it seemed as if *everything* were a crisis), her father always helped her to see things in perspective and decide what to do. He never got excited or upset the way her mother did. Oh, Linda loved her mother, too. But her father was the one who was always steady and reassuring. She would miss his strength.

But now it's time for me to start discovering my own strengths, Linda thought. *I'm going to need them.* Starting off in a strange city in a new high school with no friends would never be easy. But it would be especially hard in New York. Of course, her aunt Catherine and cousin Kim would be there. Linda would be staying with them in their apartment on East Seventy-second Street in Manhattan. She was glad she'd have them to turn to.

Linda had always looked forward to the times when her aunt Catherine and Kim had come to visit her family in Kansas. Kim was a year older than Linda, but the two girls had always gotten along very well. In fact, they had become such good friends that it was hard for Linda to think of Kim as a cousin. She was almost like a sister. Linda thought back to Kim and her aunt Catherine's last visit to Kansas City. Her father had spent all day making a kite so the girls could fly it in the field behind the house. The gesture had meant so much to Kim, especially

3

since her own father had died when she was only five.

A wave of fear and homesickness suddenly gripped Linda, but she tried to ignore it. *After all*, she thought, *haven't I already done a lot of things I was afraid of?* Leaving home was the hardest thing she had ever done, but she also knew she had to do it. Her high school in Kansas just didn't have the courses she'd need to develop her considerable artistic potential. Kendale High was a good school, but it had a very small art department that was equipped to teach only the basics. The School of Art and Design in New York, however, had amazing studios and teachers who specialized in just about every medium. Mrs. Tynes, the teacher at Kendale who had first noticed Linda's artistic potential, had told her about it. She was also the one who had encouraged Linda to develop her talents and to become an artist. Mrs. Tynes had helped Linda apply to Art and Design and had written a letter of recommendation to the school's dean for her. She had been a friend as well as a teacher, and Linda would miss her.

There were a lot of people she was going to miss. Her best friend, Amanda, was number one—except for her family, of course. She and Amanda had grown up together—they had lived just a block apart. Linda had shared everything with Amanda, from clothes to homework to—well, even a boyfriend once. They had had a fight about Todd because Linda thought that he was coming on to Amanda, but Amanda hadn't even known that Linda liked Todd. Everything had worked out fine in the end, though. They'd both learned something about how dangerous jealousy can be to a friendship and decided never to let a boy come between them again. Even a boy like Todd.

The plane was descending faster now. Linda could see the ground below them getting closer and closer. A giddy feeling came over her as she waited for the thump of the wheels on the runway. *I am about to begin a new life*, she thought. She smiled, thinking about all of the adventures that lay ahead of her.

Suddenly the wheels touched the ground with a bump, and Linda heard a loud whine as the engines reversed thrust to slow the plane down. They taxied along the runway for what seemed like forever to Linda. She wanted to get out of the plane and into the city that lay across the East River. She felt confined, and her anxiety was driving her crazy! Finally, the plane shuddered to a halt and the passageway leading to the terminal was connected to it.

Linda smoothed out as many wrinkles as she could from her flowered cotton skirt and tied her yellow sweater around her shoulders. She reached up and pulled down her beige canvas carry-on bag from the overhead compartment and headed down the aisle with the other passengers. The friendly flight attendant stood at the door saying goodbye to everyone, but she had a special smile for Linda. She took Linda's hand, squeezed it, and said, "Good luck again. I know you'll do just fine here."

Linda smiled in return and said, "Thanks. It's good to hear that, especially coming from a real New Yorker!"

There was a blast of fresh air where the door connected to the passenger ramp, and it felt good as it blew across the back of her neck. The passageway opened onto the arrivals lobby, which was crowded and noisy. Linda looked around the spacious room trying to spot her aunt Catherine and Kim, but she didn't see them anywhere. She wasn't sure whether she should wait there for them or go downstairs to the baggage area. Since she couldn't remember where they had agreed to meet, she stood still as the crowds thinned out. Still, there was no sign of her aunt and cousin.

Linda was about to take the escalator down to the luggage area when she heard Kim's voice call out from behind her, "Linda! Linda, we're over here!"

Linda turned around and saw Kim rushing toward her. Her aunt Catherine was close behind. The first thing Linda noticed was that Kim's beautiful auburn hair was short now, much shorter than when she had seen her in April. She also had short, wispy bangs that curled around her forehead. Kim's dark brown eyes lit up as she ran up and put her arms around her cousin. Linda hugged her back, standing up on her tiptoes since Kim was a few inches taller than she was. Then Linda turned and hugged her aunt Catherine.

"Let me look at you," her aunt said as she tenderly brushed a wisp of golden blond hair away from Linda's face. Her aunt's voice was light and whispery as she stood back to get a good look at Linda. She was wearing a royal blue business suit with a simple beige blouse. It seemed such a contrast to the more relaxed clothes Linda was used to seeing her wear when she visited Kansas. But even in a suit, her aunt Catherine didn't look the least bit formal or forbidding. Her soft hazel eyes had tiny creases near the edges, making her look as though she laughed a lot—as she did. "How was the flight, dear?" her aunt asked.

"Oh, it was fine, just fine," replied Linda happily. "I met a really nice flight attendant on the plane, and she told me all about New York. She says I'm going to do just great here."

"Good," Aunt Catherine said in a positive tone. "That's a good omen. How is your mother?"

"She's fine. So is Dad. Mom said to tell you she sends you lots of X's and O's."

"X's and O's. That's hugs and kisses," said Aunt Catherine, laughing. "Your mother always used to say that."

"It's going to be wonderful having you here," Kim broke in. "We've fixed the den up into a bedroom for you, and it looks great. I designed it myself," she said, taking a slight bow. The three of them laughed and Kim continued, "No, really, it looks terrific and I did decorate it myself. I took pictures of it and used it as a model for my summer school interior design class. I haven't gotten my grade yet, but don't be surprised if you find yourself sleeping in a room that gets a B-plus or better."

Linda was happy that Kim was already attending Art and Design. She would be a junior while Linda would be starting her sophomore year. Kim had promised to introduce Linda to all her friends. She had even told her about some of them in the letters the two had been exchanging over the last year. Linda looked forward to meeting them, especially Kim's best friend, Kristen. One of Kristen's paintings had won a blue ribbon in the state-wide art competition the year before. Kim had sent Linda a poster that had been made from the painting, along with a letter saying that she hoped that Linda and Kristen would become good friends, too. Kristen's painting had amazed Linda. It was so well developed and so expressive for an abstract work. But it had also intimidated Linda, and it made her feel anxious about her own work. Linda had always wanted to be the best, and Kristen's work was about as good as anything she had ever seen by a student. She knew she had her work cut out for her if she ever expected to be as good as Kristen was.

The three women had made their way down to the baggage area, and finally Linda's luggage appeared on the revolving carousel. They picked it up and went out to the front of the building to wait for a taxi. After standing in line for a couple of minutes, the three of them were seated in the back of a cab heading into Manhattan.

Chapter Two

The traffic was light going into the city, much to the delight of the cab driver. He kept up a one-sided conversation with his passengers, talking about everything from the traffic to the weather to the Yankee game the night before. Linda's aunt nodded and said "uh-huh" every now and then. But instead of making it clear to the cabbie that they didn't want to talk, her vague replies only made him talk even more. Kim and Linda found his rambling monologue amusing, and they tried to stifle their giggles in the backseat.

"What is he talking about?" Linda asked Kim between laughs.

"Who knows?" Kim replied. "Most cab drivers like to talk. I guess they do it to keep from getting bored. But you don't have to listen if you don't want to."

"This is a strange city," Linda said, shaking her head.

"You're not in Kansas anymore, *Dorothy*."

The reference to the line from *The Wizard of Oz* was a running joke between the two girls.

The cab drove across the Fifty-ninth Street Bridge, which took them over the East River and into Manhattan. From the bridge, Linda got a good look at the city that would be her home. It was only eleven o'clock, and the sun was moving so that soon it would be directly overhead. It reflected brightly from the sides of the tall skyscrapers that sat huddled together on the crowded island. How could so many people live in such a crowded place? Linda wondered. Compared to the suburb of Kansas City where Linda had grown up there were no open spaces, except for Central Park, of course. Kim had told her stories about Manhattan, but they'd seemed like just that to Linda—stories. *Now*, she thought, *I'm going to see it all firsthand.*

The cab came off the bridge, then looped around and headed up First Avenue. Linda's aunt interrupted the driver's monologue—he was commenting on how his aching knee always correctly predicted when it was going to rain—to tell him that he should keep to the left and turn the corner onto Seventy-second Street.

11

The driver pulled up in front of a large gray building with a blue awning. A doorman in a blue-and-gold uniform came up to the cab and opened the door. As they got out, Kim said, "Hi, Marley. This is my cousin Linda. She's from Kansas, and she'll be going to school with me this fall. She's staying with me and my mom."

"How do you do, Miss Linda," he said with a distinct British accent. He then turned to load the luggage the cabbie had left on the sidewalk onto the cart he'd brought out from the lobby.

Linda looked at Kim with raised eyebrows and a wide smile. She turned back to Marley and said, "Fine, thank you." *A British doorman,* she thought. *Just like in the movies.*

The three of them walked into the large, marbled lobby of the apartment building, where another man took over the cart. They rode the elevator up to the twentieth floor, turned down the corridor, and stopped at the door marked 20-G. Linda's aunt pulled a set of keys out of her purse and opened the three locks on the door.

"How come you have so many locks?" asked Linda.

"This is New York," Kim replied. "Everybody has a lot of locks on their doors."

Once inside, Linda looked around. The apartment seemed small to her, but Kim told her that it was really pretty big for the city. "You're just used to your house in Kansas City," Kim told her. "This is considered tons of room for New York City."

The hallman put Linda's bags down in the living room, and Kim's mother thanked him as he left.

"Let me give you the grand tour," said Kim as she started to lead Linda around the apartment. "This is the living room, of course," she said, gesturing with a wave of her arm around the room. "Mom designed and decorated it. Sometimes she brings clients over to show them."

Linda looked around the beautifully appointed room. It had thick, light blue wall-to-wall carpeting. The pale yellow wall behind the long, off-white sectional couch seemed to come alive as the sun's rays hit it. It looked like a room that Linda had seen photographs of in a magazine once. When Linda mentioned this to Kim, her cousin replied, "It could have been this very room. It's been in magazines a couple of times."

Aunt Catherine was an interior decorator, and one of the best in the city. But even though the room was perfect, it still had a lived-in look. There was a pile of newspapers on the glass-topped coffee table, and Linda could see the laces of Kim's sneakers peeking out from behind the easy chair in the corner. As beautiful as it was, the room was also a real *living* room, and that made Linda feel more at home.

Kim led Linda down a long hallway with a highly polished wood floor that ran from the living room to the bathroom.

"That's Mom's room," Kim said as they passed the first door on the right. The door was only half-open, and Linda couldn't really see what it looked like inside. She noticed only that the rug on the floor was white, and there was a dressing table with a green skirt that reached to the floor.

"Now this is *my* room," said Kim as they walked a little farther down the hall. She pushed the door open, and they entered. Linda stared in disbelief. It looked as though a tornado had swept through Kim's room only moments before. Clothes were scattered on the floor and heaped on the back of the chair, and record jackets lay spread about the whole room—along with books and various odds and ends.

"*You* want to be an interior designer?" Linda asked in mock horror.

"That's what Mom always says, too," Kim answered with a light laugh. "But I like it this way. It's comfortable, and believe it or not, I know where everything is."

"I don't believe it," said Linda.

"Oh, and look what I got this year," Kim exclaimed. She went over to her desk and took the cover off a computer. There was a gray-green video screen and a disc drive next to a separate keyboard pad.

"That's great," said Linda.

"Isn't it? I use it to design room layouts for class. They can be stored in the memory, and then I can call them back and make changes whenever I want to, even in 3-D. The printer's over there," Kim said, pointing to the small plastic machine on the far table. "I pulled all A's in my design courses last year. Mom had promised me that if I did, she'd split the cost of a computer with me. She keeps a bargain."

Kim went back over to where Linda was standing and said with obvious excitement, "Now let me show you your room."

They walked across the hall to another, smaller room. The white walls looked freshly painted, and there was a bed, a desk, and a small dresser with a mirror above it. A green throw rug lay on the polished wood floor.

"I know it's small," said Kim, "but it makes good use of the space. I hung rectangular posters on the walls to create the illusion of depth." She gestured to the walls. "And I painted them white because it makes the room look brighter." Kim looked at Linda expectantly. "So, what do you think?"

"I love it," said Linda as she looked around the room. "Thanks for working so hard on it. It's absolutely perfect."

They went back to Kim's room, and she turned on the stereo. "Isn't this record great?" said Kim. "I just got it yesterday, and I've already played it to death."

Linda listened. "I've heard that song," she said. "I heard it on the radio yesterday afternoon. I like it, too."

Linda sat down on the edge of Kim's bed and kicked off her shoes, feeling more at home with each passing minute. She noticed a photograph lying on the bed. "Who's that?" she asked Kim, picking it up and studying the boy's face.

"Oh, that's Shane," Kim said. "Shane Harley. Gorgeous, huh? He sings and plays guitar in a band called *The Shining.* I know him from school. The band is really hot, too. *Serious* rock 'n' roll!"

"He sure is gorgeous," said Linda.

"I'll introduce you to him if you want."

"I'd like that," said Linda.

"Well, don't get your hopes up too high," said Kim. "He's not exactly starving for attention from girls."

Linda could see why. Shane had wavy blond hair that fell to his shoulders and curled around his ears. His face looked wise and sensitive—as though he knew some secret everyone else hadn't learned yet. He was wearing a dark cotton jacket with padded shoulders over a light-colored T-shirt. But his eyes were what fascinated Linda. It seemed as if he were looking right at her. *I wonder what color they are*, Linda thought as she gazed at the black-and-white photograph.

"Actually, you'll meet everybody tonight," said Kim, breaking into Linda's dreamy thoughts. "I thought we could go down to Bleecker Street once you get settled in. Shane and the band are playing there tonight, and everyone's coming."

"Tonight?" Linda asked, a little surprised. She hadn't expected to meet Kim's friends so soon.

"Sure," said Kim. Then, trying to ease Linda's fears, she added, "Don't worry. I've got some things you can wear if you want, and everyone's dying to meet you. We'll show you how to rock 'n' roll New York style!"

"Great," said Linda, feeling less afraid. Her first night in New York was going to be a good one, she told herself. And from then on, they were all going to be good.

Chapter Three

Linda spent the rest of the day unpacking her suitcase and putting her clothes and art materials away. She arranged a few picture frames with photographs of her parents and Amanda on the desk and the nightstand. There was even a picture of Moose, their golden retriever. Having pictures of those she loved made the room feel more friendly, more like home. Later her aunt Catherine made dinner for the three of them—a pot roast with noodles. Her own mother often made the same thing, and the meal reminded Linda of home. Except for the salad. Kim had made it from exotic vegetables that she had picked up from a Korean green-grocer down the block.

The sun cast a warm orange glow in the living room that evening. Shortly after they'd finished dinner, Kim said, "We'll leave in about an hour, OK? The show starts at eight-thirty at this place called Pat's, so we'd better start getting ready now."

Linda went into her room and tried to decide what to wear. But nothing seemed right. She was going to be meeting Kim's friends for the first time that night, and she wanted to make a good impression. She didn't want to look like someone straight off the farm. Then again, she didn't want to overdo it and seem as though she were trying too hard, either. After a few minutes, she decided that the best thing to do was to see what Kim was wearing and decide from there.

Linda peered in the door to Kim's room. Her cousin was stroking on a touch of mascara. Turning toward Linda, she said, "It's more fun to get there a bit before the band goes on so we'll have time to sit around and talk to everyone."

Kim was wearing a pair of tight jeans and a loose cotton sweatshirt that had brightly colored flowers painted all over it. She had pulled her short hair back with combs on either side.

"I came in to see what you're wearing. I thought it might help me decide what to put on."

Kim noticed her nervousness. "Don't worry, anything's fine," she said. "The important thing is to be comfortable. Do you want to borrow something?"

"I've got plenty of clothes," Linda explained, "but they're the things I wore in Kansas City. When we went out back home, everybody always just wore jeans and sneakers, even to clubs."

"So wear jeans and sneakers," Kim replied. "I am. I'm sure they'll look great on you. And I've got an oversize white shirt that'll look terrific on you. It'll show off your tan. And if you want, we can go shopping for clothes and stuff tomorrow. I know just where to take you, too. In fact, we can get some ideas tonight. There are tons of great stores on Bleecker Street that are open late."

"Great," said Linda.

While Kim helped her mother put away the dinner dishes, Linda put on her favorite pair of jeans and Kim's white shirt. She slipped her feet into the new purple sneakers she'd bought in Kansas City a few days earlier. They had been her one extravagance. Then she sat down at the desk and used it as a dressing table. She was about to get up when she decided to put on a bit more mascara. *After all, this is New York,* she said to herself.

Linda turned to face the full-length mirror on

the back of the bedroom door and studied herself. She still had a deep tan from the midwestern sun. Her golden blond hair reached to the small of her back, and it was parted neatly down the middle. She played with it for a moment, trying to pin it up or back. Briefly, she wondered if she should get it cut—she'd had it long forever. *But this is me,* she thought, *and I want people to like me for who I am.*

After combing her hair one last time, Linda went into the kitchen. Kim looked at her and said, "You look fantastic! Honest. And I love the purple sneakers."

Her mother smiled in agreement. "You do look awfully pretty, Linda," she said approvingly.

Turning to Kim, she said, "Now, I want you two to be home by eleven tonight, OK?" Kim nodded. "Good. Have you got enough money to take a cab both ways?"

Kim checked her colorful straw purse. "Uh-huh. And I'll get paid the day after tomorrow."

Kim was referring to the summer job she had in a small clothing store a few blocks away. Linda asked her about it as they were waiting for the elevator.

"It's really been great," Kim told her. "I've gotten a chance to save some money, and I get a forty-percent discount on anything in the store.

What's even better, my boss said I can keep on working part-time now that school's starting."

"I'm going to have to get a job after school, too," Linda said. "My mom and dad gave me enough money to buy some clothes and art supplies, but that won't last forever."

"Don't worry," said Kim, "we'll find you something. Maybe you could even get a job in an art-supply store. There are plenty of them around school, and that way you'd be able to get discounts on all your paints and brushes and stuff."

Linda smiled. "That's a great idea."

Marley held the front door open for them and then turned on the red light above the canopy that signaled cab drivers to pull over. A yellow taxi came up to the curb almost immediately, and the two girls got in. "Bleecker Street and La Guardia Place, please," Kim told the driver.

As the cab rolled down Second Avenue, Linda stared out the window at the buildings flying by. There were so many people on the streets, too. Whenever the cab stopped for a traffic light, Linda could hear people's conversations through the open window. *So much goes on in this city,* she thought. *I don't know how I'm ever going to get used to it.*

Suddenly Kim pointed out the window. "Look at that crane over there," she said. "It's got to be at least twenty stories tall."

Linda looked at the towering maze of tubing and cables.

"There's a saying in New York that this will be a nice town if they ever get it finished," said Kim with a laugh.

"You mean that by the time I figure out where everything is, it's not going to be there any-more?" Linda asked, a little worried.

"That's the way New York is," said Kim. "It's always changing. But don't worry, it's not hard to find your way around once you get used to it."

Linda sat back in the seat and thought about what Kim had said. She felt the same mixture of courage and fear that she'd felt on the plane earlier that day. But she put those thoughts out of her mind for the moment. The night was going to be fun, and that was all she wanted to think about.

Chapter Four

The cab pulled up on the corner of Bleecker Street and La Guardia Place in Greenwich Village. Kim paid the driver and left the change as a tip. Linda looked around in amazement. She had heard a lot about the Village from friends back home who had visited New York and from Kim. Now she was right in the middle of it. There were lots of people who looked about her age walking through the crowded streets.

In fact, the School of Art and Design was not far from where they stood. It was in SoHo, the area below Houston Street that was famous for its art galleries and large, airy lofts where artists lived. Kim had told Linda about SoHo, and she was looking forward to going down there every day for school.

The two girls walked west on Bleecker Street for two blocks, passing the brightly lit shops and small, distinctive restaurants that lined the street on either side. Linda could hear the music pouring out into the street from clubs with names like The Bitter End and Preacher's. Then they turned left onto Sullivan Street and walked a few doors down to Pat's. It had a wood-and-glass front and a narrow flight of concrete stairs that led down to the entrance.

Pat's was one of the clubs in the area that catered to young people. It served soft drinks and fruit juices, along with burgers, fries, and a different "house special" dessert each night. Pat's was one of Kim's favorite places, she told Linda, because the crowd was always fun and the music was always good.

Inside Pat's, the jukebox was playing one of Linda's favorite songs. Red- and white-checkered tablecloths covered all the tables, and small candles gently flickered on most of them. There was sawdust on the floor, and a small stage was set into the back wall of the club.

Once her eyes had adjusted to the dim light, Kim saw her friends. She called out to them, and they waved Kim and Linda over to their table.

They sat down, and Kim turned immediately

to the girl next to her. She had long blond hair and a thin, angular face. Linda thought she was very beautiful, with her high cheekbones and huge blue eyes.

"Kristen," said Kim, "I want you to meet my cousin, Linda."

"Nice to meet you," Kristen replied in a quiet voice. She was dressed in black from head to toe. Her narrow pants were tucked into floppy black boots. She also wore a loose-fitting, black cotton T-shirt and several large silver rings on her fingers. The effect was a stark contrast to her pale complexion. She *looks* like an artist, Linda thought. Linda said hello to Kristen and held out her hand. But Kristen was slow in taking it, as though shaking hands was something one didn't do. Linda felt a little awkward. Kristen gave her a small, tight smile but said nothing. She finally took Linda's hand, but only briefly.

Then Kim introduced Linda to the other kids who were gathered around at the table. There was Amy, a short girl with very fine brown hair and wire-rimmed glasses. She was friendly right away, giving Linda a big smile as if to make up for Kristen's lack of enthusiasm.

Next to Amy was her boyfriend, Paul. Paul had curly brown hair almost the same color as

Amy's. He was tall and broad shouldered, and Amy looked tiny and fragile next to him. Kim told Linda he played football at his high school, DePolo.

Then there were Jerry and Tammy. They were both students at Art and Design, too. Jerry was concentrating on the graphic arts, and Tammy was studying fine arts, and Linda hoped they would be in some of the same classes. They were both very friendly right from the start, standing up to move their chairs so that Linda and Kim could sit down.

Jerry turned toward Linda. "So, have you been in New York for long?"

"No. Actually, I just got in today. We've been going nonstop," she said, nodding to Kim.

"How do you like it so far?" Tammy asked, pushing her streaked blond hair out of her face.

"I love it, even though I haven't seen very much," said Linda. "I think I'm going to like it here."

"It's a great place," said Amy in her high-pitched voice. "I've lived here all my life, and I don't think I'll ever leave."

"Except for Paris," Paul said with a grin.

"Right, except for Paris," said Amy, smiling up at him.

"She's had this thing about Paris ever since I've known her," Paul said to Linda.

"Architectural design," Amy explained. "It's what the French do best, better than anyone else. Le Corbusier is my idol, and I want to study at the Sorbonne after I graduate in two years. It's all I've ever wanted to do."

"France is OK," said Kristen in a low, husky voice, "but Europe is dead artistically. It's all been done before. China will be the next great center of modern art and design."

Then she turned her back to the table and watched as the club soundman set up the stage.

Linda shot Kim a questioning look, but she just shrugged and smiled. Soon, both Linda and Kim got caught up in the swirl of conversation at the table. The club began to fill up around them. Waitresses moved from table to table taking orders. Kim went over to the jukebox, put in four quarters, and made her selections. When she came back she told Linda, "I put on Bryan Adams. I could listen to him all night."

"So could I," said Amy. "He's got great hair. And the best eyes, too."

"Shane's aren't bad, either," Kim said in a teasing voice. Tammy and Amy agreed but Kristen didn't, Linda thought; she seemed so serious—so brooding. But her paintings were incredible. Linda had wanted to talk to Kristen about art, but she seemed so distant and unapproachable, that Linda didn't dare.

She looked up and noticed there were more people up on stage. The lights were dimmer up there than in the rest of the room, so Linda couldn't see anyone's face. But she could see that several of the people were picking up guitars. The red pilot lights of the amplifiers burned like fiery pinspots from the stage. Then the band members began to tune their instruments. Linda could hear the notes of the guitar and then the methodical pounding on each drum as the drummer adjusted its tension.

Linda was a bit startled when she heard the first drum notes. They were sitting at a table very close to the stage. But then the sound of the band tuning up began to make Linda feel more excited. Videos were great and all, but nothing compared to the experience of watching a band play live. Her eyes were riveted to the stage as she watched the shadowy figures roam across it. It was almost like *being* in a video, she thought.

Finally the jukebox rumbled to a stop as someone behind them pulled the plug. There was a hiss as the sound system was turned on. Then the voice of an announcer came up over it. "Good evening, everyone, and welcome to Pat's. Now I hope you'll all put your hands together and give a big welcome to The Shining."

One guitar began a series of chords alone as the lights on the stage came up. Then the drummer joined in, and he was soon followed by the keyboard player. The music seemed incredibly loud to Linda—and it had just begun.

A small spotlight by the soundboard came on, shining a bright beam of light on the lead singer, who had a guitar slung over his shoulder. Kim leaned over to Linda and shouted, "That's him. That's Shane."

He looked as handsome as he had in the photograph. He was holding the microphone with one hand, while the other one rested on the neck of his guitar. One of his knees was pointed out toward the audience, and he rested his weight on the other one. Shane was wearing black jeans and an old T-shirt that looked as though it had once been navy blue.

His voice was powerful, but at the same time it was melodic. It had an emotional quality that held Linda's attention as he sang.

The world doesn't care who I am
But I look at you and know you understand
I'm reaching out to you so take my hand
Together we can run.

Linda tapped her foot to the rhythm, but kept her eyes on Shane as he sang. As loud as the band was, she could understand every word as if she already knew the song. And every now and then it even seemed as though Shane was looking right at her. But Linda knew that with the bright lights in his eyes, it was impossible for him to have picked her out. Just the same, she felt a little thrill every time his eyes turned in her direction.

After the second chorus, Shane stepped forward slightly to do his guitar solo. His guitar soared sweetly and delicately over the other instruments, yet with a power that made Linda want to jump up and dance. Shane's fingers moved across the strings quickly and, it seemed, effortlessly. Then he flew back to the microphone and repeated the chorus:

I got a heart like a rebel
You know that it's true
And I can take on the whole world
As long as I got you.

Linda felt her heart pounding in her chest, as though it, too, was keeping the beat. All the kids at the table were drumming their fingers or tapping their feet to the music.

Finally the band went back to the long chords that they had played at the song's beginning, slowing gradually until at last they all came to rest on one last chord, which rang out for a long moment and then ended abruptly. It was over.

Actually, it was just beginning, Linda realized. They had only finished their first song. *How will they keep up that kind of energy for the rest of the night?* she wondered.

But somehow it happened. Incredibly, the band got better and better the more they played.

After about eight or nine songs, the band bowed to the audience and ran off the stage. The soundman called for them to come back and take a bow, and the audience joined in, chanting Shane's name over and over. Finally the band walked slowly back onto the stage.

Shane walked up to the microphone and said, "We'd like to thank you all for coming out tonight and being here with us. We hope you enjoyed it as much as we did. Thanks a lot!"

Then the band launched into one more song, a really fast one that started everyone in the room clapping. When they finished, they left the stage while the audience again called for more. But they didn't come back this time.

Linda watched Shane as he walked down the aisle between the tables, heading toward the dressing room. As he disappeared from view, she sat back in her chair, feeling almost as drained and tired as the band members.

Kim leaned over and touched Linda on the shoulder.

"Isn't he everything I said he was?" she asked.

Linda nodded. "And more," she agreed. *Much more*, she added silently.

Chapter Five

The seven of them stayed at the table after the show. Even Kristen smiled a little now and then and seemed a little warmer than she had before the show. She hadn't said anything directly to Linda, but she didn't appear to be quite so standoffish, either.

Linda listened to everyone, occasionally asking questions about New York or school. Since everyone at the table was going to Art and Design except Paul, she got lots of advice about classes, teachers, and other things.

"If you're interested in painting, you should try to get into one of Miss Caro's classes," Tammy told her. "Everyone I've spoken to who's had her says she's great."

"I've heard the same things about her," said

Amy. "I might even take a course with her next semester."

Amy turned to Kristen. "Didn't you have Miss Caro last year?" she asked.

Kristen nodded. "Yes, I did. She's good."

Amy paused as if she expected Kristen to say more, but Kristen just looked down at the flickering candle. Amy raised her eyebrows slightly and turned to Linda with a shrug.

Kim got up to go to the ladies' room a minute later, and Linda went with her. Inside the cool, tiled room, Kim said, "Kristen's really not as distant as she seems. She's just—different, that's all."

"I'll say," Linda replied. Then she added, "I guess I did kind of feel as though she was looking down on me. I mean, here I am, fresh off the plane from Kansas, and Kristen looks so— well, she looks so *sophisticated*."

"Don't be silly," Kim said. "Everyone likes you. Tammy, Amy, everyone." She paused and looked into the mirror thoughtfully. "It's just that Kristen is—oh, how can I put it? Kristen is shy in a funny sort of way. Even though she looks really confident, she's not. She doesn't warm to people right away. It takes her time. But"—Kim turned to her cousin—"I want you to like her, so at least give her a chance. I felt the same way about Kristen when I first met her. But after I got to know her, I saw that she's an amazingly sensitive person. I know you two will end up friends."

Linda thought about what Kim had said for a moment and then said, "I want to like her, too. And I know from the poster you sent me that she's an incredible artist. But"—Linda paused—"I hope she gives me a chance, too."

"She will." Kim smiled and touched Linda's shoulder. "Come on. I'm dying of thirst."

When Linda and Kim got back to the table, Amy and Jerry were discussing other teachers at the school, commenting on them and their classes. But after a few minutes Linda was only half listening to them. She found herself glancing over at the jukebox and the dressing room door just beyond it. People were walking in and out of the dressing room, including some members of the band. A waitress walked in with a tray full of sodas and left with an empty one a minute later, tapping it against her leg as she walked.

Linda wanted to get another look at Shane. She watched as several people went into the dressing room. Linda wished for a moment that she could get up and go into the dressing room herself. But, no, she could never do a thing like that. It was silly to even think about it. Linda shook her head. She had only been in New York for a few hours, and she was already day-dreaming about visiting a rock star in his dressing room. Well, Shane wasn't exactly a star—he didn't have a video or even a record out. But he did seem to be something like a star around there, at least. *And he certainly deserved to be one*, Linda thought.

Linda turned back to the table and listened as Jerry described the math teacher he had last year.

"Don't let them put you in Pederson's math class if you can help it," he said. "That guy makes your life miserable. He's got it in his head that he's going to turn everyone into an accountant. I think he feels that because he teaches at an art school, he has to push us harder or we'll end up being great artists who can't add."

Tammy and Amy nodded in agreement. Linda made a mental note to stay away from Mr. Pederson. Tammy looked as though she was about to say something else to Linda, but instead she glanced up over Linda's shoulder and said, "Oh hi, Shane."

Linda was startled. She turned around quickly and saw him standing right next to her. Her eyes widened. She felt herself starting to blush and turned away.

Shane gave Kim a friendly smile, and then turned to greet the rest of the group. "Great show!" Amy exclaimed enthusiastically.

"Thank you," Shane replied, bowing with great ceremony. Then he looked over at Kristen. Their eyes met for a second, but she turned away and faced the stage.

The atmosphere was tense for a moment, but then Kim spoke up. "Shane, there's someone here I'd like you to meet."

Linda felt her heart pounding in her chest. It was as if *she* were about to go onstage herself.

"Shane," Kim continued, "this is my cousin from Kansas, Linda Wills. Remember I told you about her? She'll be living with my mom and me for a while."

She told him about me? Linda thought, shocked. What had Kim said? Linda turned in her seat and looked up at Shane shyly. He smiled at her, and she grinned back. Linda noticed that his eyes were blue.

"Hi, Linda," Shane said. His voice was warm and friendly. "Welcome to New York. I'm glad you could come and see the show."

"Your band is really great. It sounds so"—she realized she sounded a little too eager—"good."

"Thanks." Turning to Kim, he whispered loudly enough for Linda to hear, "You didn't tell me your cousin was such a knockout."

Linda blushed even more than she had before. She even felt a bit embarrassed by the remark. But at the same time, it made her feel warm inside.

Kristen stood up and headed toward the ladies' room by the side of the stage. As she passed Shane, she shot him a withering stare. Shane watched her as she walked away, then he turned back to face Linda.

"I'm sorry," he said, "did you say something?"

She looked at him quizzically and shook her head. "No."

"Oh, I must be hearing things." He looked down at her and added in a soft, serious tone, "I'm glad I got to meet you tonight. I hope I'll see you again soon."

Linda nodded. "I'll be down again the next time you're playing. Kim and I both will."

"I hope I won't have to wait that long," he replied. Shane then winked at Linda and said goodbye to everyone at the table.

As soon as he was gone, Kim leaned in toward Linda. "I think he likes you," she whispered dramatically. But then she burst into giggles, and Linda knew she was kidding.

"Don't worry," Kim said, still laughing. "I'm only teasing."

"So was Shane," Tammy added.

Linda was confused. She looked over at Kim.

"Look, what I meant was that Shane is, well—he knows a lot of girls. And he can be very friendly," Kim explained. "But he doesn't usually mean anything by it. I guess he's what you'd call a charmer. Just don't take anything he says seriously."

Linda turned at the sound of Kristen's voice. She must have come back to the table while Linda was talking to Shane. Now Kristen smiled and said, "I've got to get going. I'm really tired. See you guys at school." She got up and walked out the front door into the night.

"Kristen can be weird sometimes," Tammy said.

"I agree," Amy chimed in. "I mean, we're all studying to become artists, but Kristen seems to think she is one already. The way she only wears black and stuff. Weird."

Linda looked over at Kim, who said nothing.

Tammy and Jerry got up from the table. "We've got to get going, too," said Tammy.

"Amy and I should be on our way as well," said Paul.

"In other words, you've got a curfew, too,"

said Kim, laughing. Paul nodded. "That's OK. So do we."

Kim looked over at Linda and then down at her watch. "It's ten o'clock. Come on, let's take a walk down Bleecker Street and I'll show you some of the shops before we have to head back uptown."

Once everyone was outside, Linda said good-bye to Tammy, Jerry, Paul, and Amy, adding that she was glad she had met them. They all told her they'd see her when school started the following week, if not before.

Paul said, "I won't be seeing you quite so often, unless you want to transfer over to DePolo High."

Linda laughed. "Maybe next year, but I'm going to give Art and Design a chance first."

"Well, if you ever want to play football, DePolo's the place to go," he said.

Everyone laughed. Then the group split up. Tammy and Jerry headed west toward Sixth Avenue, and Paul hailed a cab for himself and Amy. Kim and Linda waved to them all and turned back up Sullivan to Bleecker Street.

As they rounded the corner, Linda noticed that the streets were still pretty crowded even though it was getting late. Music poured out from the open doors of the clubs that lined the street from one end to the other. It was still warm, but there was a gentle breeze with a slight chill to it. Linda wished she had thought of bringing a sweater.

As they walked, Linda thought about Shane— and Kristen. What had happened between them to make her so cool toward him? She looked at Kim. "What's the story with Kristen and Shane?" she asked.

"Well, remember when I said that Shane knows a lot of girls?" Linda nodded. "Well, sometimes he can say things to you that he really doesn't mean. And he always sounds so sincere that you really want to believe him. I think Kristen believed in him a little too much. She kind of pressed him for a commitment. I'm not exactly sure what else went on. Kristen doesn't talk about it, even to me."

"Shane seemed to mean what he said tonight," Linda argued.

"He probably did," Kim replied, trying to smile. "Look, I just wanted you to know what he's like so you don't get your hopes up."

Linda thought about Kim's warning. Remembering Shane's eyes and the sensitive look in them, Linda couldn't believe Shane wasn't telling the truth. Why would he lie, anyway? Still, Kim's words rang in Linda's ears. She knew she'd have to be careful where Shane was concerned.

Suddenly Kim stopped and said, "Here's one of those shops I was telling you about." She pointed at a dress in the window. "Isn't that gorgeous! It's the kind of dress you want to go in and try on, even if you know you can't afford it."

Linda looked at the dress. It had a lace collar and a wide, flowing skirt. The price tag on the bottom read one hundred and nine dollars.

"It's so expensive!" Linda gasped.

"Everything in New York is expensive," Kim replied with a short laugh.

They continued down the street, looking into the store windows as they went, stopping every now and then to comment on a dress or skirt that one or the other of them liked. Every store seemed to have its own style. It wasn't just the clothes, either. Each one had its own kind of atmosphere, from the color the walls were painted to the lighting effects. Everything had been carefully designed to create a distinctive mood.

They passed another club as they neared Sixth Avenue. Linda heard someone playing an acoustic guitar inside, and she paused in front of the door to listen. The tune was softer and more reflective than the music Shane's band had played. The contrast pleased Linda.

She peered inside and saw the guitar player. His head was bent down as though he was thinking about something very sad. Then he looked up, leaned toward the microphone, and began to sing.

> *There's a heart that is empty*
> *Just as empty as mine*
> *It's looking for someone*
> *Someone hard to find*
> *Could it be you*
> *Could it be you.*

His voice had an aching note in it, as though the words were coming from deep inside him. Linda didn't know quite why, but she wanted to stay there for a few more minutes and listen to him.

Kim, who had continued walking when Linda had stopped, turned around. "Hey, what's the matter? What are you doing?"

"I just want to hear this musician play for a minute, that's all," Linda said.

Kim walked back over to Linda. She looked in the door at the guitarist. "Oh, that's Tom—Tom Hagen. I really like his songs. They're a lot different from Shane's, though. I mean, he's not exactly rock 'n' roll."

Linda listened for a moment longer and then turned to Kim. "Could we go inside and listen to him? Just for a second?"

Kim looked at her watch. "It's almost ten-thirty, and Mom said—" Kim shrugged. "Well, just for a couple of minutes. Sure, why not?"

Chapter Six

The place was called simply The Bleecker Café, and it wasn't nearly so crowded as Pat's had been. Linda and Kim sat down at a table in the middle of the room. A waitress, who had been leaning against an iron railing near the far wall, came over and took their soft drink orders. Then they sat back and listened.

No, Tom Hagen wasn't anything like Shane. Shane generated a sense of excitement that was obvious from the moment he picked up his guitar. Even so, Tom's music affected Linda greatly. There was something in his voice that made her want to listen to it, to listen to what he had to say. He sounded sincere and honest— as though he believed each word he sang.

When the song ended, everyone in the small

club applauded politely. Tom smiled and said, "Thank you all for coming down tonight. This is Bill Smythe on the piano and that's Fred Meyer on bass. My name is Tom Hagen, and we'll be back a little later for another set. Hope you can stick around for it."

The audience applauded again as the three of them stepped down from the stage. Bill and Fred walked past the table where Linda and Kim sat. When Tom passed by, carrying his honey-colored acoustic guitar with him, Kim reached out and touched his arm.

"Hi, Tom," she said with a friendly smile.

Tom stopped and looked down at Kim. "Hi. I haven't seen you in ages. Thanks for coming down."

"We were just over at Pat's," she told him.

"I heard Shane was playing there tonight," he said.

"He was great," said Kim. She turned to look at Linda. Facing Tom again she said, "I want you to meet my cousin. Linda Wills. Linda's from Kansas, and she's going to Art and Design this year."

"Hi, Linda," Tom said. "How are you doing?"

"Fine, thanks," she replied. "I really liked your last song. We came in at the end and only heard that one, but it was very pretty. You have a good voice."

"Thanks." He turned to Kim. "Thank you for bringing her down tonight. Compliments are always welcome."

"Don't thank me," Kim said with a smile. "We were walking past the club when Linda heard your voice. She made me stop."

Tom looked over at Linda. His dark, tousled hair fell in curly locks over his forehead. He had chocolatey brown eyes and long, dark lashes.

"Well—uh, thanks," he said. "That's a nice compliment coming from a girl like you. I mean—a girl as pretty as you are." He smiled awkwardly.

"Thank *you*," said Linda, feeling a bit awkward.

"You know, I'll be playing down here again in a few weeks," he said. "Maybe you could come and hear a whole set next time. I'll let Kim know in advance so she can tell you."

"You can tell her yourself at school, Tom," said Kim.

"You go to Art and Design, too?" asked Linda, a bit surprised.

"I know," he said with a laugh, "everyone forgets about Art and Design's performing arts programs. I guess the name is sort of misleading. But Art and Design has some great music courses. I'm studying classical guitar and music theory. What are you studying?"

"Painting. I want to be an artist," said Linda.

"And people have told me that I have the talent it takes to be good." She paused, looking into Tom's kind brown eyes. "Of course, I know I've got a lot of work to do before I can call myself a real artist."

"I like painting," said Tom. "I'm afraid I'm not very good at it, though. But I took Miss Caro's class last year, and she helped me a lot. She's a good teacher. You should try to get her if you can."

"I've heard about her," said Linda. "I'd like to get into her class."

"I'm also studying writing," Tom added. "It helps me with my music."

"Did you write that song we heard?" Linda asked.

Tom nodded. "It's awfully hard. Most people think that a song just pops into your head fully formed, but they're wrong. They don't understand how much work you have to put into a song, how much of yourself goes into each word and note. It's as hard to write a good song as it is to write a good book, or to paint a good landscape."

"I never thought about it like that before. How do you decide what to sing about?"

Tom hesitated for a moment. "Well, to begin with, you shouldn't write about things you don't know about. If you do, people can tell you're not being honest with them. So I just write about how I feel, people I know, things I've done—that kind of thing."

Tom looked a little embarrassed at having said so much. He stared silently down at his guitar.

Kim broke the uneasy silence. "It's getting late, you guys," she said. "Mom said eleven, and even if we get a cab right away, we're still not going to get home in time." She asked the waitress to bring them their check.

"You're right," said Linda. "I didn't realize how late it was." She turned back to Tom. "It was good to meet you. I hope I'll get a chance to hear more of your songs sometime."

They said their goodbyes, and the two girls paid for their sodas and walked back out into the street. They walked west to Sixth Avenue, where Kim raised her arm over her head and waved to a taxi coming up the street.

"Seventy-second and First, please," said Kim to the driver as they got in. "And could you hurry, please?"

The cab sped off, heading uptown to Fourteenth Street, and then over and north up First Avenue.

"What a long night!" Kim exclaimed. "I'm surprised you're not asleep on your feet. It's been a big day for you."

Linda sighed but managed a smile. "Yes, but it was exciting, too. I guess I'm just overtired." She turned toward Kim. "You know how you get when there's so much going on that your body forgets to tell your brain that it's exhausted?"

"I know the feeling," said Kim. "It gets reversed at finals time—your mind gets tired but your body's so tense from worrying that it won't let you go to sleep."

"I don't think I'm going to have any trouble sleeping tonight. I may not even bother taking my shoes off."

"I don't think that's such a good idea," Kim said with a laugh. "But I know what you mean."

Streetlights seemed to fly by as they went, and the buildings along First Avenue became dark blurs in the night. The moon was a shadowy silver crescent hanging in the blue black sky above Manhattan, fighting to be seen against the bright lights of the city below.

The cab finally pulled up in front of their apartment building. The night doorman came out and opened the rear door of the cab as Kim paid the driver. She gave him an extra large tip because he had driven them home so quickly. Then they raced to the elevators. Kim anxiously shifted her weight from foot to foot as they waited. After what seemed like an eternity, the doors finally opened.

When they reached the twentieth floor, Kim and Linda hurried down the hall. As Kim was fiddling with her keys—"I can never remember which one is which," she complained—her mother opened the door.

"Well, good morning, ladies," Linda's aunt said with disapproval. "You two are a bit late, aren't you?"

"It's my fault, Aunt Catherine," Linda explained. "I asked Kim if we could stop at another club for a moment to hear a musician. I'm sorry, it won't happen again."

"I'll overlook it this time," her aunt said, her tone softening slightly. "But let's try to stay within the limits in the future, hmm? School starts on Wednesday, and you're going to have to get up pretty early from then on." Her frown turned into a smile.

"Yes, ma'am," Linda said.

"OK. Off to bed, you two."

"OK, Mom," Kim replied. She headed straight for her room, Linda following close behind her.

As Linda brushed her teeth, she began to feel the effects of her long and tiring day. It took all her energy just to get undressed and pull back the covers on her bed. She folded her clothes over the back of the chair and set her shoes near the closet door. Then she lay down on the soft mattress and pulled the covers up to her neck. She reached over and turned off the lamp on the nightstand. Her aunt called out from behind the closed door, "Good night, dear. Sleep well."

Linda wished her a good night and then rolled onto her side and fluffed the pillows beneath her head. She felt her eyelids begin to close, but her mind was still churning, reviewing everything that had happened. She thought about what Tom had said about how you have to use the things you know about in your art. *That's what art is all about,* she thought.

Her mind shifted to all the other people she'd met that night, who had said what and so on. It was all a blur except for Tom's words. *It's too bad he's so bashful,* Linda thought. *Since what he's saying is so true.*

She turned on her other side, trying to relax and fall asleep. All the new faces and names jumbled together in her mind, but the last person she thought about before she drifted off to sleep was Shane.

Chapter Seven

The next several days were hectic ones for Linda. She had less than a week to get ready for school, and there was so much to get done. Kim took her shopping for clothes and art supplies, and they stopped at school so she could double-check her registration and choose her elective classes. And just when Linda began to think she had done everything, she'd remember something else she had to do. With all the running around, though, she was starting to get to know New York a little better. She had learned which way each avenue went, as well as how to find her way around her new neighborhood.

But the streets of Greenwich Village baffled Linda. Unlike most of the city, which was laid out in a grid of parallel streets and avenues, the Village was a maze of streets that crossed at odd angles. Many of the streets had unfamiliar names, like Horatio, McDougal, and Waverly Place. And even some of the avenues that were numbered uptown took on different names when they reached the Village—Eighth Avenue became Hudson Street, for example.

Taking the subway was a shock, too. Back in Kansas they drove wherever they needed to go. In Manhattan, hardly anybody that she had met had a car. Taxis were fine at night, but they got expensive if you took them all the time. So Linda learned the subway routes she'd need to get from the Upper East Side down to the School of Art and Design, which was located a couple of blocks south of Houston Street in SoHo. Her subway stop was the Houston Street station of the Seventh Avenue line.

Linda was a little scared about taking the subway at first. She had heard stories about how dirty it was and how easy it was to get lost. But with Kim's coaching and a subway map, she got used to it pretty quickly. It wasn't really frightening at all. Still, Kim told Linda to be careful about whom she spoke to, and Linda took the warning to heart.

The first day of school would be disorienting.

Kim would be with her on the way to and from school and on breaks during the day, but they weren't in any of the same classes. Luckily, Linda met Cindy, another painting student on the way to school the first day. Cindy had attended Art and Design as a freshman the year before, and she helped Linda find her way around. Cindy's ears had perked up as soon as Linda had mentioned that she hoped to get into one of Miss Caro's classes.

"She's the best!" Cindy agreed. "All summer I've been looking forward to having her. But it might be tough to get into her class this late. A lot of the kids like her."

Linda hoped there would be an opening, but since she hadn't been able to choose her electives the previous spring the way everyone else had, she didn't get her hopes up too high. As soon as she entered the building she went to the head of the art department's office. There Mr. Caleb said, "I know you're a transfer student this year and didn't get the opportunity to pick all the elective courses that you would have liked. Normally you wouldn't have gotten into a class as popular as Miss Caro's. But"—he smiled at her—"Miss Caro has apparently had her eye out for you. It seems she received the portfolio that you submitted when you first applied here. She was quite impressed with your work, and asked me to keep an eye out for you. When your application for her class came across my desk, I called her. She's made room for you in her fundamentals of painting class."

Linda was thrilled. She remembered what her aunt Catherine had said about good omens when she had first arrived in New York. *Maybe omens count for something after all,* she thought.

Once her schedule had been settled, Linda felt more relaxed about things. Her first meeting with Miss Caro came the next day. The class was absolutely packed. When the teacher called her name during roll call, she looked up and smiled. Miss Caro smiled back at her.

Miss Caro was a round-faced woman with large green eyes and long, sensitive fingers— artist's fingers. She was stern, but that was tempered by the close personal attention she gave to each student. She asked everyone in the class to draw basic shapes and figures on the first day, evaluating the good points and shortcomings of each one, one at a time.

After class that day she asked Linda to stay for a minute after everyone else had left. She pulled out the drawings that Linda had submitted in her portfolio and looked at them while Linda stood quietly beside her. Then she turned around to Linda and said, "You know, Miss Wills, this is very, very good work for someone your age. I'm very impressed. You have a good eye for balance and depth, but your sense of color needs to be developed a bit."

As Miss Caro spoke, Linda felt nervous and happy at the same time. She was glad that Miss Caro had singled out her work, but at the same time she wondered if that would make it harder for her. After all, she did have very high standards. It was going to be hard to live up to them.

"I know that your move to New York was probably one of the biggest things in your life," Miss Caro continued. "And I know you must feel very pressured about being here. You strike me as someone who expects quite a bit from herself. These paintings show a remarkable attention to detail." She paused, took off her glasses, and looked at Linda. Her features softened as she spoke. "This is a difficult school," she said. "I want you to know that my standards are even higher than the school's. When I come across someone with your kind of potential, I try to give that person special attention. In thirty-five years of painting and teaching, I have learned how to spot talent. And I never let talent go to waste. I'll see you tomorrow, Linda."

Linda was happy as she left the room. She met Cindy in the hall on the way to her next class.

"What did she want to talk to you about?" Cindy asked.

"She thinks I have talent," said Linda. "It made me feel good, but I know that I'm going to have to work extra hard in her class. She made me feel that having talent is a responsibility."

They walked down the hall and split up when they reached the stairs, each heading to her last class.

"See you tomorrow," said Cindy.

"OK," Linda called back. "See you in home-room."

After school that day, Linda went to meet Kim at the door to the school cafeteria. She was waiting there with Tammy and Amy.

"Hi, Linda," said Tammy. "How do you like school so far?"

"It's great," Linda replied. "It's going to be a lot harder than it was back home, though. But then I guess that's what I came here for."

"You're going to learn a lot just by living in New York, too," Amy added.

"What's going on in the cafeteria?" Linda asked, noticing all the activity inside the large room.

"Tammy and I are helping some of the se-niors decorate the cafeteria for their party this weekend," Kim said. "Too bad we won't get to go, though."

"I'm just waiting for Paul," Amy explained, looking at Linda.

Suddenly there was a sharp screech over the PA system. The group turned and saw Tom stick his head out from around the corner. "Oops, sorry," he said with a smile. "I'm setting up the sound system for the party, and I guess I forgot which switch was which."

Tom walked over to where the girls were standing. "How did we ever get roped into helping the seniors out, anyway? We're doing all the work, and they get to have the party." Tom was talking mostly to Kim and Tammy, but he kept stealing glances at Linda. He still appeared to be a bit shy around her, and Linda was surprised to realize that she felt a little shy, too. Tom was so quiet and gentle—somehow Linda felt awkward being her normal, outgoing self in front of him.

Just then, Paul walked up to them. He said hello to everyone and gave Amy a quick kiss on the cheek. "Practice was canceled today because the coach is sick. So, in honor of my free afternoon, how would my favorite girl like to go to the movies?"

"I'd love to," Amy answered enthusiastically.

"Anyone want to come along?" Paul offered.

"Sorry," Tom said. "I've got to get back to that sound system."

"And we've got to get cracking on those decorations," Tammy added, pulling a rolled scarf around the top of her head to hold her hair back.

"We'll only be about another hour," Kim said, turning to Linda. "If you wait, we can go home together."

"Sounds good to me," Linda said. She opened her art history book and started reading.

By the second week Linda was beginning to feel more comfortable in school. One afternoon after class she met Cindy on the front steps of the main building. She started telling Cindy about her life back in Kansas and how she was still trying to adjust to New York.

Cindy nodded sympathetically and told Linda about how she and her family had moved to Manhattan from Brooklyn two years earlier. "Brooklyn's not that far away," said Cindy. "I mean, it's only just across the river. But moving was still a big change for me. Brooklyn has all these neighborhoods that are like little worlds of their own. You get to know everyone who lives on your block, and people are always ready to help their neighbors out. Now I live over in the thirties on the East Side. I have to come down here for school and over to the Upper West Side for my clarinet lessons. I really miss having everything together in a real neighborhood."

"I know what you mean," said Linda. She was glad to have found a friend who understood how uprooted she felt. As they continued talking, Linda and Cindy pulled out some of the recent sketches they'd done for their art classes. Cindy was just putting hers back into her red nylon backpack when Shane and two other boys came out the door behind them and down the concrete steps. They were talking and laughing, but when Shane saw Linda, he stopped. "Hi, Linda," he said to her with a smile. "You guys go on ahead," he told his friends. "I'll meet you at the record store up on Bleecker." His friends waved, and one of them gave Shane a wink and a grin.

Cindy stood up, pulling her backpack over her shoulders while Linda just stared at Shane.

After a long, tense silence, Shane turned to Cindy. "Hi, I'm Shane Harley. You must be a friend of Linda's."

Cindy smiled and seemed to blush a little. "Yes," she said in her soft, girlish voice. "I'm Cindy. Linda and I are in homeroom together." Then she turned to Linda. "I've got to get going. I'll see you tomorrow."

Linda was putting her sketches in order, fumbling because her hands were shaking slightly out of nervousness. As Cindy left, Shane called out after her, "Nice meeting you." He flashed her a broad smile, and Cindy smiled back and waved as she walked down the street.

Shane then turned back to Linda and said, "What have you got there?"

Linda said, "Oh, nothing, really. Just some drawings I've been working on."

"Could I look at them?" he asked.

Linda hesitated a moment. Then she showed him a drawing of an old horse barn and a fenced pasture. Her pencil strokes were light and feathery in places, bold and thick in others. They really made the scene come alive.

Shane stared at the drawing for a few seconds and said, "This is great. I didn't know you were so talented."

"Thanks," Linda said shyly. "Miss Caro has already helped me so much. I never could have done something like this before."

Shane handed the sketch back to Linda. "You know, we really have a lot in common. I mean, we're both artists—though not in the same way." He thought for a moment, his blue eyes dancing with enthusiasm. "We both create something beautiful that wasn't there before—you through your drawings and me through my songs."

Linda listened as Shane spoke, not knowing what to say. To her, art was also taking something and making it more beautiful. That was a kind of creating, she supposed. She started to think of a way to say that to Shane, but before she could open her mouth he said, "I'd really like to see more of your stuff one of these days, but I've got to run now. I have to meet the guys from the band. I'll see you around school."

He smiled at her and then walked down the rest of the stairs. Linda wanted to go with him, but she knew she couldn't. Instead, she watched as he walked slowly and gracefully down the sidewalk. *He thinks I'm an artist. Well, yes, that is what I am—an artist.*

When Linda got home, Kim was getting ready to go out. She wanted to tell her cousin about meeting Shane after school, but the doorbell rang before she could speak. "That's Kristen," said Kim. "We're going up to see an exhibit at the Metropolitan Museum, and she's late."

Kim opened the door to let Kristen in. As usual she was wearing black from head to toe. That day she also had on a black beret, which made her look even thinner and more severe. Linda politely said hello to her, but Kristen just looked at her and raised her hand in a limp wave. As Kim was pulling on her jacket she said to Linda, "Sorry I've got to run. I'll see you when I get home, OK?"

"Sure." Linda sighed, figuring her news could wait a few more hours.

Kim ran out the door with Kristen ahead of her. "Tell Mom I'll be back by suppertime. I'll see you then."

Linda watched as the door closed behind them. She smiled as she went into her room and sat at the desk. *It's been a very special day,* she thought. *Very special!*

On Friday afternoon Linda and Kim were talking about Shane as they walked across Houston Street, heading east to Broadway to meet Amy and Tammy. Linda had told Kim about her talk with Shane a few days earlier, and now they were trying to decide which one of his songs they liked the best. As they passed a small, blacktop basketball court, they heard someone call their names. They both turned and saw Tom, who was running beside the wire fence that surrounded the park. On his way he passed the basketball back over his shoulder to one of his friends.

"Hi, Linda. Hi, Kim," he said, leaning against

the fence as he caught his breath. "Where are you guys off to?"

"Linda and I are going over to Broadway to do some window-shopping," Kim said. "Want to come with us?"

Tom laughed. "No. Mike and I bet Jeff and Andy that we could beat them one-on-one in thirty points. The losers have to buy the winners lunch all next week."

"Coming with us would be more fun," Kim said teasingly.

Tom looked over at Linda and said, "Maybe, but I'll take my chances."

"Well, if you're sure. You could use a new sweatshirt, you know," Kim replied.

They all laughed at Kim's remark. Tom touched the torn collar of his shirt. "Hey, this is in fashion right now!"

Kim shifted her books in her arms. "Linda, Amy and Tammy are waiting for us." She paused. "Hey, if you two want to talk, I'll meet them and we'll wait for you." Kim winked at Linda and then ran off up Houston Street. She didn't wait for a reply.

There was an awkward silence as Tom leaned on the fence and Linda kicked some stones around with the toe of her sneaker. Then they both began to speak at the same time, their nervous words running together and making them both laugh.

"Well," Tom finally said, "how's school so far? Are you getting used to living in New York?"

"It's tough sometimes," Linda admitted. "It's so different from Kansas City. But I do like it here—especially the music," she added with a grin.

"Thanks," said Tom simply.

Linda smiled at him. He looked so handsome, standing there in his shorts and a sweatshirt. His dark hair was damp and tousled from the exercise.

"How's the music coming?" she asked him.

"Oh, it's going OK, I guess. I've been working pretty hard on a couple of new songs."

"It's not easy being an artist, is it?" she said, thinking for a moment about Shane.

"Well," Tom replied, "I've got a way to go before I can really call myself an artist. I'm still learning the essentials."

"Essentials are sort of the building blocks, right?" said Linda. "I mean, that's what being an artist is all about, isn't it? Creating things that never existed before?"

"I don't know if I agree," Tom said. "I'm always changing my definition of what art is. Right now I think it's taking what you have and making it as good and beautiful as you can."

Linda realized that that was exactly what she wished she could have said to Shane the other day. Tom had put it so perfectly.

She was trying to think of what to say next when a crash next to them shook the fence. The basketball bounced away slowly, and Tom looked over his shoulder at his friends, who were waiting impatiently. "Come on," his friend Mike called. "I don't want to have to pay for lunch all next week because you were too busy gabbing."

Tom looked back at Linda. "Sorry," he said. "I have to get back to my game. Maybe we can get together again soon."

Linda looked at him with a slight smile. "I'd like that," she said. "I have to get going, too. Kim and the others are probably wondering what's happened to me."

She headed down Houston Street, walking quickly. She looked back and shouted to Tom, "See you around." Tom waved back to her before picking up the basketball.

Chapter Eight

By the beginning of October, Linda felt confident that she could find her way anywhere she had to go—from SoHo to the Upper East Side, even to Chinatown. Linda also felt much more comfortable in school now that she had been there almost a month. One brisk afternoon she and Kim were walking up Bleecker Street after school. They had planned to do some shopping in the boutiques that lined the street, but when they got to Sullivan Street, Kim stopped. "Let's go check the schedule at Pat's. Shane told me the other day at school that The Shining was going back to play there soon."

Linda had seen Shane around the school a few times over the past few weeks. He always said hello to her in the halls, but he usually seemed to be in a rush to get somewhere. He still had a mysterious air about him that attracted Linda and made her want to get to know him better. Not to mention the fact that he was gorgeous. Linda was thinking about his brilliant smile as she and Kim walked toward the club.

They peered into the club's darkened window. The bright afternoon sunshine reflected off it, making it hard to see the hand-lettered schedule. Finally they saw the band's name, which was penciled in for Friday, October sixth.

"That's this Friday night," said Kim. "I hope we find some cute clothes today so we can wear them to the show."

"Me, too," Linda agreed. "I saw a pair of black pants in the window of Jump the other day that I want to go in and try on. They were only twenty-two dollars, and they'd look incredible with that red sweater I bought last week."

They walked back to Bleecker Street and over to the black-and-white-fronted store with JUMP printed on the windows in black slashes. Linda found that the pants she had seen were even on sale.

She pulled the pants off the rack and folded them over her arm. "I'm going to the dressing room to try them on," she said to Kim.

"Oh, Linda, I forgot to tell you something," Kim said. "I saw Tom Hagen yesterday when I was walking past the music department. He told me that he's playing over at the Bleecker Café this weekend." She peeked over the door at Linda. "He wanted me to make sure to tell you to come. He said it twice," she said with a conspiratorial grin.

"Great. We'll see both Shane and Tom," Linda said. "If there's time."

After dinner on Friday night Kim and Linda dashed into their rooms and began getting ready for the evening. Every few minutes, one of them would run in and ask the other for advice on her hair or clothes.

Linda kept playing with her hair, but it never seemed to look the way she wanted it to. She tried wrapping a scarf around it as Tammy did, but the scarf just looked silly on her. Then she tried tying it back, but that didn't look right either. Finally, she ran into Kim's room to get her to help. Sitting on Kim's bed, she noticed the photograph of Shane lying half hidden beneath a stack of records. In the excitement of getting ready, she had almost forgotten that she would be seeing both Shane and Tom that night. She was excited, but also a little nervous. Both Tom and Shane had shown a bit of interest in her—Tom in his shy way, and Shane more directly. She thought about how different the two boys were. *How can I like both of them?* she wondered. Then she shrugged. *Why not?*

Linda asked Kim to try anything with her hair. Kim used two barrettes to pull the sides back, leaving a spray of wispy bangs across her forehead. Linda liked the look.

At seven-thirty when they were finally ready, they went into the living room to say goodbye to Kim's mom. "You two look lovely," she told them, brushing a strand of Kim's dark hair out of her face. "Have a good time tonight. And remember, I want you home by eleven."

"Oh, Mom," Kim said, "can't we make it eleven-thirty tonight? It's kind of a special occasion, and we've been keeping up with our homework and all."

Her mother thought for a moment. "Oh, all right—eleven-thirty. But not one minute later."

The two girls smiled, then ran out the door and down the hall to the elevators. Marley saw them coming through the lobby and turned on the taxi call-light.

"It looks as though you two are going out for a big night," he said.

"We sure are, Marley," Kim said. "It's going to be a rock 'n' roll night."

Marley smiled at them and opened the door of the cab that had pulled up in front of the building.

Ten minutes later they were in front of Pat's. They walked down the steps and inside. Amy and Paul were waiting for them by the jukebox.

"Hi, guys," said Paul. "Tammy and Jerry called me before we left. They said they'll be a little late."

"Is everything all right?" Kim asked.

"I think so," Paul replied. "Tammy sounded pretty happy over the phone."

They all walked to the next room, where they sat down at a large, round table. Tammy and Jerry walked in about twenty minutes later.

"What happened to you two?" asked Paul. "When Tammy called she didn't say much besides the fact that you were going to be late."

Jerry spoke as he and Tammy sat down. "My sister called from California this afternoon. She's getting married."

"Susan's getting married?" said Amy. "That's wonderful news. When? To whom?"

"This guy she met at the preschool where she works. We met him when they came East over the summer. He's really nice. Now my mom and dad are making arrangements to fly out and see them, and things around the house have been nuts since they called. The wedding's going to be sometime in April."

"That's really terrific," said Kim. "I really like your sister. Give her my congratulations when you see her."

The conversation at the table revolved around Jerry's sister's wedding for a while. Linda felt like part of the group now. She knew everyone better and saw them in school every day. She felt comfortable with them, and even though they were a year older than she was, it didn't seem to matter. Still, Linda wished Cindy had been able to come. It would have been nice to have one of her own friends there.

After a while Linda turned to Kim and said, "Where's Kristen tonight?"

"She didn't want to come," said Kim. "She said she wasn't feeling well, but I know it's because she didn't want to see Shane."

"She still doesn't talk about him, does she?" asked Linda.

"I told you, Kristen's not like most people," Kim said. "Shane's just one of those things she doesn't like to talk about. She knows that I'm there if she needs me, so I don't push her about it."

Tammy started to say something when Amy shouted, "There's Shane!"

Linda turned around and saw him walking toward their table. She felt her heart start beating faster the closer he came.

Shane pulled up a chair from another table—right next to Linda. His arm brushed against hers as he sat down.

"Hi, Shane," Kim said. "Did you guys do your sound check and all?"

He nodded. "It sounded really good." Then he turned to Linda and in a quieter voice said, "Sorry I haven't had the chance to talk to you lately. But I've been thinking about you. There's a new song in the set tonight that I think you'll recognize when you hear it."

Linda wasn't sure what to make of his remark. Why would she recognize one of his songs? He sounded as though he was going to sing a song that would be special to her. What could he have meant?

"Hey," Shane said, looking around the table, "I have some news. Remember that tape we made three months ago?" Everyone nodded. "Well, we finally heard from the record company we sent it to." He paused, smiling like a Cheshire cat.

Finally Kim said, "So, don't keep us in suspense. Tell us what happened."

"They liked it!" he said at last. He leaned

forward and clasped his arms. "They not only liked it, but they also said that if the rest of the songs are as good as the three on the tape, they might be interested in doing an album!"

"Shane, that's wonderful!" Kim exclaimed.

"That's terrific," Amy added.

"Congratulations," Jerry said.

"And . . ." Shane said, turning to Linda once again, "I think that the new song we're doing tonight is going to be one of the tunes that gets us the deal."

He winked at her, then got up from the table. "I have to go to the dressing room and get ready," he told them. "I'll see you guys after the show."

As he left, Linda thought about the night ahead of her. Shane had singled her out for some reason, and that made her happy. She knew that something was about to happen. She didn't know what, but it had to be something great.

Just then Linda saw Cindy come in the door. "Cindy," Linda called, waving her hand. "Over here."

"Hi, Linda," she said when she got to the table.

"But I thought you said you couldn't come tonight," Linda said.

"I didn't think I'd be able to at first. I was getting behind in my homework, so my mom grounded me. But after you told me how good this band was, I knew I had to hear them. So, I worked a little harder this week and did a little pleading. What can I say—my mom can't say no when I beg."

Linda introduced Cindy to everyone at the table. Moments later the lights in the room were dimmed, and the jukebox rumbled to a halt.

"Ladies and gentlemen," the announcer said, "Let's have a big hand for The Shining with Shane Harley."

The room erupted with applause. *So,* thought Linda, *Shane now gets his name mentioned along with the band's. He really is a star.*

The band's amps roared into life with the opening to the first song, "Heart like a Rebel." Shane looked great standing up on the stage. He was wearing jeans, with a gray T-shirt and maroon suspenders. As he sang, his sparkling blue eyes looked out across the room. Every now and then he'd glance at Linda, and she felt a tingle each time.

The small stage made Shane seem larger than life. Although there wasn't much room, his movements were fluid and easy—graceful. He would jump around on the stage, mugging with the other band members, and then move back to the front of the stage to look into the audience. Linda was amazed at what a knowledgeable performer he was. The focus of the entire audience was on him.

The set was going well, each song better and more powerful than the last. Then, the fifth song into the show, Shane said, "Here's a new song I just wrote. I think it's our best one yet."

The band began to play a sweet, simple introduction. Shane played a few chords on his guitar, then stepped up to the microphone and began to sing. His voice was soft and low.

The song was about an artist. *He knows I'm a painter*, Linda thought. *I wonder . . .* She listened to the lyrics.

You came into my cold life
And you filled it with your art
You've made my life so perfect
Now that you're here in my heart.

Linda was really excited now. Shane was singing about her! He had to be. As Shane started into the chorus, he looked right at her with his piercing blue eyes. They seemed to see right through to her soul.

"It's almost as though he's singing about you,"

said Cindy, leaning over to speak into Linda's ear.

Linda barely heard her. She was completely lost in Shane's song. All she heard was Shane singing to her, singing about her. She'd never felt anything like it before. It was as if time were standing still and there was nothing else in the world except Shane and her.

The audience loved the song, too. There was a huge thunder of applause after the last chorus. Linda wished the moment would never end, that it would go on forever and ever. But they launched into another song after the clapping had died down, and the spell was broken. Still, Linda knew that she'd have the memory of it forever.

When the show ended, Linda watched Shane and the rest of the band head into the dressing room. She also saw some of the same girls who had been there the first time go in. She wanted to go and see Shane, too, but she couldn't bring herself to do it. *Why hasn't he come out yet?* she wondered. Why was Shane staying in there with those girls, after he had just sung that song to her?

Finally Linda couldn't stand waiting anymore. She stood up and excused herself. Just as she got to the jukebox, Shane came out of the dressing room. He headed straight for her, his beautiful eyes looking directly into hers. He reached out to take her hand and drew her into an alcove.

"I didn't know any other way to do it," he said, his voice still deep and husky from singing. "I knew there was something special about you from the moment I saw you. Then I saw the drawing you had done in school that day, and I knew I wanted to get to know you better. It inspired me to write that song. It's one of the best things I've ever written, and I couldn't have done it if I hadn't met you."

Linda felt herself melting inside. She looked up at his kind, gentle, handsome face. His eyes—those blue, blue eyes—sent a shiver down her spine.

"But I didn't dare just come right out and say anything to you," he continued. "Expressing my feelings in a song seemed easier somehow." He touched her cheek gently. "You're not like the other girls I know. They all try so hard to be something they're not. They put up fronts and try to act older. I guess they think that makes them more attractive, but it doesn't. At least not to me."

He pulled her close to him and rested his chin on the top of her head.

Linda was swept away by Shane's words, and she didn't want to break the spell by saying a thing. Even so much as drawing a breath might shatter the magic of the moment. After what seemed like an eternity, she said simply, "It was beautiful, Shane."

Chapter Nine

The jukebox had been turned up again, and a soft, romantic song was playing. Standing there with Shane was like a dream come true to Linda. She couldn't believe that she—Linda Wills—had been chosen by a boy as handsome and sensitive as Shane.

Finally they broke apart. He led her by the hand from the alcove back toward the table.

As they made their way across the room, he whispered in her ear, "Let's not share our secret, OK? Not just yet."

She thought she understood, even though she wished she could tell Kim. But Shane probably just wanted to keep it to themselves for a while.

"Nice show," said Amy when they got back to

the table. "Those new songs were great, especially the one about the artist."

"I think you guys have that record deal locked up," said Jerry. "The only thing you've got to worry about is which song is going to hit number one first."

Everyone talked with Shane for a few minutes, but then he excused himself. "I've got to go back to the dressing room and talk about some things with the band. There's a guy in the audience tonight who said he might be interested in managing us, and we want to talk to him. He's managed other bands before and gotten record deals for a couple of them. There'll be another set in about forty-five minutes, if you want to stay for it."

He gave Linda's hand another squeeze beneath the table, and then he stood up and went back into the dressing room.

"Well, I guess Shane's really going places, huh?" Amy remarked.

Paul shook his head. "No, he's not. He doesn't even have a car."

Everyone groaned at Paul's joke. Everyone except Linda, that is. She was still thinking—or dreaming was more like it—about the events of the evening.

Kim looked at her watch and turned to Linda. "You know, it's getting a little late. I did tell

Tom that we'd stop by and see his show tonight over at the café. He goes on again in about ten minutes. If we leave now, we'll have just enough time to catch his show and then make it home by eleven-thirty."

It took a moment for Kim's words to register with Linda. Kim nudged her cousin in the side gently with her elbow.

"Hey, are you in there?" she said lightly. "Or should we send in a search party?"

Linda turned to her. "Oh, I'm sorry. I just . . ." She shook her head as if to clear away her daydreams. "I'm really sorry, Kim. I didn't hear you."

Kim put her hand on Linda's knee. "I know," she said. "That was a pretty nice song Shane wrote about you. He must really mean it."

"Of course he means it," Linda said. "Why would he do something like that if he didn't?"

Kim hesitated a second, as though she might have had an answer to her cousin's question. But instead she said, "Well anyway, what about going over to see Tom's show?"

"Oh, I completely forgot about that," Linda gasped. She turned to face her cousin and asked, "Do you mind if we don't go? I'd rather just stay here and catch part of Shane's next show. I'm sure we can hear about half of it before we have to head home."

Kim raised one of her eyebrows slightly. "I think Tom is kind of counting on seeing you tonight. I told him you'd be there."

"Well, you shouldn't have made a commitment for me without asking," Linda replied.

"I meant that *we'd* be there to see him tonight," said Kim. "And after all, you were the one who was so interested in his music. You were the one who pulled me into the club that night, remember?"

Linda said yes, she remembered, but that she really would rather stay for Shane's next set. They could always see Tom some other night.

Kim turned to the others at the table and asked them what their plans were. They all seemed to echo Linda's thoughts. They would like to catch some of Shane's next set. Cindy, however, had to go then.

"I guess I've got a stricter curfew than you guys do." She said goodbye to Linda and all the others at the table and headed for the door.

The group at the table stayed for Shane's next show. He sounded as good as he had the first time, if not better. He didn't perform "Artist" in the beginning of the show. Linda wanted to stay to hear it again, but there was no way to ask him to play it while he was onstage. They stayed as long as they could, but finally and reluctantly, she and Kim had to leave.

As they waited for a cab, Kim said to Linda, "We do have a minute or two to run over to the Bleecker Café and say hello to Tom."

Linda said, "We'd better not. I don't want to take the chance of getting home late and upsetting your mom."

Kim shrugged her shoulders and said, "OK. Let's get going then."

For the next few days all Linda could think about was Shane. The events of that night at Pat's had been so quick and unexpected, like a lightning bolt. But she couldn't get those few moments out of her mind. She found herself humming the chorus to "Artist" over and over.

And then, when Shane called her at home a week after the show and asked her out, it was as though she had been struck by *another* bolt of lightning.

She remembered each word of their conversation:

"Linda, it's Shane," he had said.

"Oh, hi, Shane," had been all she could think of to say.

"Listen, I was wondering if you were free tomorrow night. I know it's a Saturday and it's kind of late to call, but . . ."

Linda hadn't been able to believe he was asking her out. She'd felt surprised, excited, and everything in between. "No—no, I'm not doing anything, Shane," she'd said, stammering a little.

"Well then, how about a movie?" he'd asked. "There's a new one at the Sixty-eighth Street Playhouse that's supposed to be great. That's up in your neighborhood, isn't it?"

"A movie? Great!" she'd said. "I'd like that."

They had agreed on a time for him to pick her up, and she'd hung up the phone, feeling ecstatic. It had been after school when he called, and Kim was out with Kristen for the afternoon and her aunt was still out with a client. There had been no one Linda could share her excitement with, so she'd just done a little dance around the living room and then gone down the hall to her room.

The next night Linda spent hours getting ready for her date. Shane came over at seven, and Linda introduced him to her aunt. She greeted him warmly and said she hoped they'd have a good time. As they rode down together in the elevator, Shane took Linda's hand.

"You're beautiful tonight," he said softly.

"Thank you, Shane," she said modestly. She thought he looked terrific, too. He was wearing a heavy black cotton sweater and gray jeans.

The dark colors highlighted his fair coloring and deep blue eyes.

He paid for her ticket at the movies. Once they were inside, he asked Linda if she'd like popcorn or a soda. She was so nervous that she said no, even though she really would have liked some popcorn. *Oh, well,* she thought, *I could do without the calories.*

The movie was very good. It was one of those "coming of age" movies with lots of characters that Linda could relate to. Part of the movie was set in Kansas, but Linda didn't feel a bit homesick. Just being there with Shane made the rest of the world seem so far away. They watched in silence for the most part, laughing now and then. Shane would occasionally say something about the musical score of the movie, commenting on the parts that did or didn't work. Linda was amazed at his knowledge of music.

When it was over, they left the theater through a side door. "So what did you think?" Shane asked.

Linda had liked it a lot, but she wanted to say something more than that to Shane, something interesting and observant. "I thought—I thought it was really well written and photographed," she said. "And the acting was—"

"I thought the score was great," he interrupted.

"That composer has written the music for some movies before, but this was his best yet. I really want to get the soundtrack album and check it out."

They walked a little farther. Then Shane said, "I know a great place around here where we could get some dessert if you want. Do you like Italian food?"

"Italian food? Now?" she asked. "I've had dinner already, and— "

"No, no." Shane laughed. "I'll bet you think Italian food is just pasta and sauces. I'll show you."

They walked a few blocks to a small café, which had a black-and-white tile floor and pink walls. They sat down at a white wrought-iron table with matching chairs, and when the waitress came to the table Shane ordered for both of them. "Two cannolis and a couple of cappuccinos, please."

As she listened to Shane order, she thought, *He's so sophisticated. He knows everything about things like this.*

As they sat there eating their crunchy, sweet pastries, Shane told her about the possible record deal for The Shining.

"Things look really good," said Shane. "I'll know more about where we stand in a couple of weeks. These things take a lot of time, and there'll be some pretty heavy negotiations involved."

Linda could well imagine that. After all, didn't every musician want a record deal? It was the same as if they had been discussing an exhibition of her work at a famous museum or gallery. Hearing Shane talk about the deals made her think about her own career.

It also reminded her of what Miss Caro had said to her a couple days earlier in class. "Linda," she had said in her strict yet motherly way, "your work is improving. Your sense of tone and color has shown a marked improvement over these last few weeks. However," she continued, "there seems to be a certain flatness to your work lately. Some of the lines don't have that crispness that I've come to expect of you. I'm sure you're absorbing what I'm teaching you, but I don't think you're using your talent to its fullest."

Then she had put down the papers she'd been holding and said in a softer tone of voice, "Linda, is there something bothering you?"

How could anything be bothering me? Linda wanted to ask. *The most wonderful guy in the whole world loves me. How could anything be wrong?*

But Linda knew that she couldn't say anything about it to Miss Caro. She just wouldn't understand. Linda was sure that Miss Caro would just smile and dismiss Linda's feelings a trivial.

At the same time, Linda knew that Miss Caro was right—her work had been a little sloppy. But she had found it so hard to concentrate on anything recently. All she could think about was Shane. She drew pictures of him in class all day long and even considered drawing a portrait of him and giving it to him as a present. After all, he had given her a gift through his art, why shouldn't she do the same?

All Linda could give Miss Caro was a promise that she would try harder and concentrate more in the future. Miss Caro seemed to accept that.

But sitting there with Shane, it was hard to think about anything at all except him. He had told her about other clubs in New York that he and the band played in, and even some clubs in nearby New Jersey and Connecticut. For someone who was so young, Shane certainly knew what he wanted in life. Linda admired that in him.

When Shane brought her home that night, he stopped as they neared her building. Pulling her into his arms, he kissed her gently on the forehead. "I had a wonderful time, Linda."

She hoped he'd say something else—something that would tell her how he felt about her—

but he didn't. *Oh well,* she thought, *you have to give love time. Nothing worth having ever comes right away.*

They parted from their embrace and he took her to the lobby of the building. As Marley discreetly looked the other way, he gave her a last, quick kiss on the cheek and told her he'd call her the next day. She watched him as he walked off down First Avenue. She hoped he'd turn around so she could wave to him once more, but he kept on walking.

Kim was home when Linda came in. She asked Linda how her date had been, but all Linda could say before she went into her room and closed the door was, "It was great. Really great."

Shane didn't call her the next day, and she didn't see him in school on Monday or Tuesday, either. Finally on Wednesday, she couldn't wait any longer and decided to call him herself. She knew that it might not be the proper thing to do, but she couldn't help herself.

A woman answered the phone after it had rung three times. It must have been Shane's mother. When she asked to speak to him, Linda heard the woman call Shane's name loudly. There was no answer, and she called again. Finally he picked up.

"Hi, Shane. It's Linda."

"Oh. Oh, hi, Linda," said Shane in an apologetic tone.

"I just wanted to call you and see how you were doing—and to say thanks again for the other night, of course."

"Look, I'm really sorry I haven't called you," Shane replied. "It's just that things are really starting to happen with the band. It's going even faster than I'd expected. The band has to go into the studio and make another demo tape. This is the one that could really do it for us. I really meant to call you, but I've been so busy."

"That's OK, Shane. I understand," Linda said.

"Look, I'll give you a call real soon and we'll go out again. Maybe we'll even have something to celebrate the next time. OK?"

"That would be great, Shane. It really would."

They said their good-byes and hung up. As Linda put the receiver back on its cradle, she thought that no matter what news Shane did or didn't get by the time she saw him again, just *having* another date with him would be cause enough for celebration.

The next day Linda had to go over to the school's other building, which was closer to Houston Street. She rarely went over there since all of her classes were in the main building.

She had been asked by a teacher to pick up some chemicals for removing paint.

As she walked down the hallway, she felt a hand tap her shoulder. "Linda?" She turned around. "Hi, Linda." It was Tom.

Linda was taken aback for a second. It had seemed like a long time since she had seen Tom that afternoon at the basketball court.

"Oh, hi, Tom. How are you?"

"Fine. You know," he began shyly, "I was hoping that you'd have come down to see me that night at the café. Kim told me that you two would be down."

Linda felt embarrassed. "I'm sorry, Tom. I really wanted to come see you, but we got tied up and couldn't make it. You know how it is on a Friday night with a big group of people."

"I know how it is," Tom agreed. "But the show really went well that night. And the next night, too. We've been working on a couple of new songs. They're really coming together."

"That's great," Linda said. "I'd like to come by and hear them sometime. Are you playing at the café again soon?"

"Nothing set yet, no," Tom answered. He hesitated, as if he had more to say. Linda began to feel uncomfortable.

"Linda, I—well, I was wondering if you're free this weekend—I mean, I'm not playing and I was wondering if you might want to go out. We could go downtown, and I could show you some of the other clubs. There's some really great music in this town."

"Oh, I'm sorry, Tom," said Linda. "But I can't this weekend."

"Well, how about some night next week then. We could make it an early night. Just a movie or something."

"I—I don't . . ." Linda's voice seemed to desert her. Finally she said in a quiet tone, "Tom, I don't think I can go anytime. You see, I'm going out—I'm seeing somebody else at the moment."

"Oh, I didn't know," Tom said, obviously disappointed. "I didn't mean to put you in such an awkward position. But thanks for being honest."

There was a tense pause. Linda felt terrible about having had to say that to Tom. He was really a nice person, after all. But so was Shane.

Suddenly Tom reached into his pocket. "Here," he said, "this is a copy of a tape that I made a few days ago. I'd like you to hear it." He handed her a cassette.

"Thanks," she said.

"After you listen to it, I'd love to hear what you think."

"I'll let you know the next time I see you," said Linda, surprised and touched by the gesture.

"Well, I guess I'll be seeing you around," said

Tom. "I've got a class I have to get to right now."

They said goodbye and walked off in different directions. As Linda turned to go up the stairs at the end of the hall, she glanced down the corridor. She saw Tom turn around and look at her. He waved, and she waved back.

Later that day, as she was walking to the subway, Linda took Tom's tape out of her purse. She put it into her tape player and put the earphones over her ears. She looked at the cassette box. On it were Tom's name, phone number, and the titles of three songs. The first was "Love Has Its Own Kind of Time." Linda always used the little cassette player on the subways because it helped drown the noise of the trains.

The train was just arriving, and Linda had to run to get in before the doors slid shut. She found a seat, pushed the play button down, and listened. Tom's voice was as warm and rich as she remembered it. Hearing it made her think of that night in the Village when she'd first heard it waft through the September air.

The words captured exactly what she had been feeling about Shane. The song was about how love took time; how it couldn't be rushed.

Time goes so slowly
When you're waiting for the one and only

Time goes so slowly
You can feel so lost and lonely
Love has its own kind of time.

But how long do you have to wait? she
wondered. *How long did it take before you'd
know if the love you felt was real—or if it
wasn't?* Tom seemed to understand her feelings,
at least in his songs. He must have felt the same
way once. Wasn't that what he had told her—that
you can't write about what you haven't felt?

Linda suddenly felt bad about putting Tom
off like that. But what else could she have done?
She loved Shane, and he certainly seemed to
care about her. But were those feelings love?
But if he didn't love her, why would he have
written that song?

Chapter Ten

Linda began to feel anxious thinking about Shane, so she turned off the cassette player after the first song. She even almost forgot to get off at Forty-second Street to change trains. She hurried towards the doors just as they were about to close. She pushed past the crowd and made it to the platform just as the doors closed behind her.

She made her way to the platform to catch the train that would take her across town. From there, she had to get still another train uptown.

When she got home, Linda was exhausted, emotionally and physically. She had a lot of homework, but she couldn't bear to face it just then. Lying down on her bed and closing her eyes, she tried to clear her mind. If only she could sleep.

No one else was at home. Her aunt was out at work, and Kim had gone with Amy to watch Paul at football practice. The apartment felt empty. It was worse than empty—it was deserted. She wished Shane would call. She knew that what was going on in his life was important and that he was very busy. Still, he should find a little time for her, shouldn't he? It was tough being the one who had to wait all the time.

She looked over at the sketch pad that lay open on the desk. There was a line drawing of Shane that Linda had started a few days earlier on the top page. It was only a rough outline she'd done from memory, and there were areas that needed to be shaded and filled in. Linda thought about getting up and working on the drawing, but she decided not to. *Why should I do something when he's obviously not thinking about me?* she thought.

Instead, Linda picked up a book she'd been reading for her English class. She read the words, but she wasn't really paying attention to what they meant. Her mind was far away. Finally, after having reread the same sentence a dozen times without really understanding it, Linda put the book down and closed her eyes to think. In minutes she was asleep.

The nap did Linda a lot of good. It was dinnertime when she finally woke up. She felt more alert and calm.

"Has school been rough?" her aunt asked when Linda came into the kitchen.

Linda nodded, rubbing the sleep from her eyes. "With midterms coming up and all, I've had a lot of work lately. And school is a lot harder than it ever was back home. But then, that's what I came here for, right?"

Her aunt nodded in agreement. "It is a tough school, honey, but I don't think you bit off more than you could chew. Your mother said your grades were always high." She put the casserole on the table just as Kim came out of her room.

"Hi, stranger," she said to Linda as she sat down. "Where have you been hiding?"

"In my room," Linda admitted with a laugh. "I couldn't keep my eyes open when I got home from school." She didn't tell her cousin how upset she was that Shane hadn't called.

Later that evening, after they'd both finished their homework, Kim wandered into Linda's room and the two girls talked for a while. Linda told her cousin about what Miss Caro had discussed with her a few days before.

"Her criticism scared me a little," Linda admitted. "I felt as though I'd let her down. But it also made me even more determined to do well in her class. I've been paying more attention to my painting since then."

Kim picked up the sketch pad that was lying on Linda's desk.

"Not bad," she said, looking from the sketch to Linda and back again.

"It's nothing," said Linda. "I was just fooling around, that's all."

"It's pretty good," said Kim. "You've really got his features down well. I'll bet it'll look great when you're finished."

"It'll look fine," Linda replied vaguely.

"Have you seen him lately?" Kim asked in a cautious tone.

Linda looked at the floor. "About a week ago."

"Well?" Kim asked.

"Well, what?"

"Well, what's going on with you two?"

"We see each other when we can," said Linda, a trace of annoyance in her voice.

"I saw Tom Hagen today," said Kim, changing the subject. "He said he gave you a tape."

"You seem to know an awful lot about my social life," Linda shot back. She knew she was being hard on Kim, but she couldn't help it.

Kim was trying to talk about things she didn't feel like discussing just then.

"Well, I was only trying to show that I care," Kim said, the resentment in her voice plainly evident. She turned to the door and walked out. "Don't worry. I won't bother you anymore."

Linda wanted to stop her, but she couldn't find the right words. Suddenly she felt as lonely and confused as she had when she'd first gotten home. As she got ready for bed, Linda heard her aunt say good night to Kim. Then her aunt poked her head into her room. "Good night, Linda, dear."

"Good night, Aunt Catherine," Linda mumbled.

"Is everything all right?" her aunt asked after a moment.

Linda pulled the covers over her. "Everything's fine, Aunt Catherine. Just fine."

Her aunt smiled. "OK, but if you ever want to talk about anything, you know I'm here." Linda nodded, and her aunt quietly closed the door.

Chapter Eleven

Shane called Linda a week later. Just hearing his voice on the phone made up for all the days of doubt and uncertainty. He sounded so sincere when he apologized for not calling her sooner. Linda said that she understood how busy he was with the band, his record deal, and school. She asked how it was going.

"Really well," he told her. "This tape we're doing is fabulous, and I just have a really good feeling about it."

"Did you record 'Artist' yet?" Linda asked.

Shane paused. "No, not yet. We're still working on a better arrangement. I really want to spend time getting it just right." He paused again. "It's a very special song for me—for us."

Linda felt a warm thrill of happiness at his

words. Then a tiny flash of uncertainty passed over her. "You're still going to record it, aren't you?" she asked.

"Of course. We may not do it during this session, but I know for a fact that it'll be on the album," he said.

"I thought— Oh, forget it," said Linda. "So, Shane, what's up?" she asked in a bright voice.

"Well, I thought you might like to go to a movie," he said. "There's a new comedy at that theater on Fifty-ninth and Third that's supposed to be really great. How would you like to go?"

"Sure, Shane," she replied. "That sounds fine. When?"

"Tonight. At around eight?"

"Oh, Shane, I can't," Linda apologized. "I told Cindy I'd come over and study with her tonight. Midterms are in two weeks, and—"

"This is the only free time I'm going to have for a while," Shane said, interrupting her. "The band is going to be pretty busy between working in the studio, rehearsing and playing. Can't you get together with Cindy another night?"

Linda thought for a moment. Cindy was counting on her to be there, and they did need to go over the work. Getting colors just right and learning the mixture formulas were important, and they were both having a hard time with those things. On the other hand, who knew when Shane would call her again?

"OK, Shane," she said, "I'll call Cindy and tell her that something came up. I'm sure she'll understand. So you'll be over at eight?"

"Maybe it would be better if you met me at the theater. It's close to the studio and that way if the rehearsal runs a little late, you won't have to wait."

Linda was surprised and disappointed. Even though it made sense to meet at the theater, she wished he were going to meet her at the apartment instead. But then, Shane's rehearsals were important, and after all, he wouldn't have to go to them forever. He'd have plenty of time for her after the tape was finished.

"All right," she agreed. "I'll meet you at eight in front of the theater. The Coronet, right?"

"Um-hmm. The movie starts at twenty after, so eight will be perfect. I'll see you then."

"OK. Bye, Shane." Linda hung up the phone. *Well, so what if I have to meet him there. People do that all the time,* she thought.

It was already four o'clock. Linda ran back to her room to do her homework so that there would be enough time to get ready and walk down to the theater by eight. As she was poring over her math assignment, Kim came in from school.

"Hi, how're you doing?" she asked.

"Fine," replied Linda. "Can I borrow your red shoes again tonight, Kim?"

"Sure," Kim replied. "What's up? Are you going out tonight?"

"Yes. Shane and I are going to a movie over on Third Avenue."

"That's great, Linda," said Kim sincerely. "Have a good time."

"Thanks, we will. I'm sure of it," Linda said, smiling.

Kim went into her room to get the shoes. She came back in with them and a new scarf she had just bought.

"Here, you might want to wear this, too," she said to Linda, handing her the scarf.

"Wow, thanks. Oh, Kim, it's beautiful," said Linda. "I really like the colors, and it'll go perfectly with my black pants and these shoes. Thanks."

Linda ate her dinner quickly so she could go and get ready for her date with Shane.

"What time is he coming to pick you up?" asked her aunt as she cleared the table.

"He's not," Linda replied. "I'm meeting him over at the theater."

Her aunt raised an eyebrow but said nothing.

Then Kim gasped, "Oh, no, I almost forgot. Cindy gave me this book of color slides to give you. She said you forgot it in class today."

Cindy! Linda had completely forgotten. She ran into the living room and called her friend. Cindy answered, and Linda told her that she wouldn't be able to make it over that night.

"Why not?" Cindy asked. "It's really important that we get this stuff done. Neither of us is exactly a pro when it comes to color mixing."

"I know," Linda admitted, "and I'm really sorry. We'll do it tomorrow night, I promise. It's just that something's come up."

"It must be something pretty important," Cindy teased.

"It is," said Linda. Then she lowered her voice. "It's Shane. He said he can only see me tonight, and it's been so long since we've seen each other. He's the most important thing in the world to me right now. You do understand, don't you?"

Cindy's voice was reassuring. "Sure, I understand, Linda. We can get together tomorrow. Have a good time, OK? And say hello to Shane for me."

Linda smiled. "Cindy, you're great."

She hung up and rushed to her room to get ready. Later, as she ran out the door, Aunt Catherine called after her, "Eleven-thirty, Linda, and not a minute later."

Since Linda was running a little late, she decided to take a cab to the movie theater so she'd be there on time. It was an extra expense—especially considering the fact that she hadn't found an after-school job yet—but it was worth it to be on time.

The taxi pulled up to the corner of Fifty-ninth and Third just before Linda paid the driver and got out. She looked around, but Shane was nowhere to be seen. She stood in front of the theater and waited. After a while she began to worry. Maybe Shane was stuck in the studio and couldn't call her. Maybe he had called after she'd left the apartment. She looked at her watch. It was already ten past eight, and the last of the people who had been waiting in line had gone into the theater. But there was still no sign of Shane. She was just about to go find a pay phone and call home to see if he'd called there, when she saw him running down the block.

"Hi, Linda," he called breathlessly, slowing down. "Sorry I'm late."

"Hi, Shane," she said. "What happened?" she asked, trying not to sound too anxious.

"We ran late, that's all." He kissed her on the cheek, and they went inside. They sat in the back of the theater and held hands throughout the picture. Linda had trouble concentrating on the movie with Shane so close to her. He'd squeeze her hand every now and then, and a tingle would run down her spine. By the end of the movie, Shane was sitting with his arm around her while she rested her hand on his knee. As the credits began to roll, Shane looked at her and said, "Wasn't that excellent? Did you notice how well they scored the music, how it helped pace the story so well?"

"I liked it, too," Linda agreed. "Maybe someday you and the band will get the chance to score a movie. Maybe you'll even have a hit theme song like 'Eye of the Tiger.' "

He looked over at her with his deep blue eyes and said, "That's what I like about you, Linda. You aim high." He laughed lightly. "Still, you never know. If you work hard enough at what you do, anything can happen. Anything." Then he leaned over and kissed her lightly on the cheek. He slipped his arm around her waist. Linda felt a rush of tenderness toward him. How could she ever have doubted Shane? she wondered. When he was close to her, time seemed to stand still and nothing else in the world seemed to matter. If that wasn't love, what was?

As they walked arm in arm, away from the theater, Linda had an idea. She wanted to try to capture the way she was feeling at that very moment on canvas. She wanted to set down the thrill, the fear, the excitement—the intensity—of being in love. She would call it "Two Lovers." A simple title for the simplest, and also most complex, emotion in the world.

Linda thought for a moment about the word *love*. Shane had never said he loved her. *Maybe this will be the night,* she thought. She looked up into the blue black sky and focused on the first star she could see. She closed her eyes and wished as hard as she could. *Let it be tonight. Let him tell me he loves me tonight.*

They walked over to Fifth Avenue, and then uptown to Central Park. Open horse-drawn carriages carried couples through the streets around the park. They were slow and regal compared to the usual crunch of cars that clogged the street. Linda wished she could ride in one of them with Shane some night. It would be just the two of them, cuddling beneath a blanket in the backseat as they rode through the park at sunset.

"It's been a wonderful night, Linda," Shane said, stopping and drawing her into his arms. "We'll have to see each other again soon." He kissed her gently.

"What about this weekend?" Linda asked shyly.

"I can't," said Shane. He sounded disappointed. "The band has to rehearse and get ready to finish the recordings we're working on. It's important that we spend all the time we can on these songs, Linda. We may not get another chance."

But what about us? Linda wanted to ask.

"I'm sorry we can't spend more time together. I really care about you, Linda."

"I understand," said Linda reluctantly. "I know how important your music is to you."

"Good," Shane said. "I was afraid you'd be angry. Well, I guess I'll get you a cab now. I'll call you when I get a chance."

"But—"

"I have to go back home and finish that song I was writing," Shane explained.

Linda couldn't resist the look in Shane's eyes. She realized that she'd just have to be patient. He hailed a passing cab and as she climbed in, he kissed her quickly on the cheek. As the cab pulled away from the curb, Linda gave the driver her address. Then she turned around to wave to Shane. But he was looking in the other direction for another taxi and he didn't see her. Linda suddenly felt a wave of loneliness. As she stared out the cab window, a single tear slid down her cheek.

Chapter Twelve

A few days later Kim and Linda were sitting with Tammy and Amy in the cafeteria eating lunch. They were all eating sandwiches or salads—except for Tammy. Tammy had a plastic container in front of her that contained beautifully arranged portions of Japanese food—rice rolled in seaweed with fish or vegetables in the center, and small, cream-colored dumplings in a brown sauce.

"Leave it to Tammy to eat sushi," said Amy, "when she could be having a sloppy joe or something."

Tammy smiled. "Do you have any idea what's in a sloppy joe? Or worse, what it does to your insides? This food"—she pointed to her plate—

"is healthy food. It's good for you, and it tastes good, too."

"I'll stick with chicken sandwiches," said Amy.

"Same here," added Kim. "A hamburger never hurt anyone," she said, biting into her sandwich.

"Where I come from, people think there's something wrong with you if you don't like hamburgers," Linda added.

Everyone laughed. When they were done eating, Amy and Tammy excused themselves and hurried off. Linda and Kim sat at the table across from each other, leisurely finishing their sodas. Kim looked up after a while and said, "I saw Tom earlier today."

Linda's gaze met her cousin's. "Oh?" she said. "How is he? I haven't seen him much recently."

"He's fine," Kim said. "He's busy with his music. And you know he's working in the PA room making the music tapes that play on the system during breaks."

"Sounds like he's been busy."

"Yes, I guess he has," said Kim. "He asked about you, though. He wanted to know how you were doing and all. I said you were busy as everyone else with midterms. I told him he should give you a call and ask you himself."

"Did he say he would?" Linda asked.

"He said that he'd catch up with you at school."

"Did he say anything else?"

"Just that you told him you were seeing someone—and that he figured it was Shane. I said I didn't think that it was serious—"

"Of course it's serious," Linda interrupted.

"I meant that I thought that you two weren't going steady right now and you'd probably see other guys if someone asked you."

Linda didn't say anything.

Kim continued. "I think Tom feels that he can't compete with someone like Shane. Not that Tom isn't great, but he seems to think that Shane's too tough an act to follow."

"What did you say?" asked Linda.

"I told him that there's more to a relationship than just being glamorous."

Linda leaned back in her chair. "Kim," she said in a low voice, "I'm not sure what to do. I like Tom, but I care a lot for Shane, too. I love Shane, and I think he loves me, too."

"Did he tell you that?" Kim inquired.

"No," Linda admitted. "Not yet."

"Well, it's your decision, but don't shut Tom out—at least not until you're sure about Shane."

"Thanks, Kim," said Linda. "I won't."

Kim looked at her watch. "The bell's going to ring any second, and I've got to get to English class and finish some homework before it starts.

I've got to work tonight, so I'll see you later at home. OK?"

"OK." As Linda hurried up the stairs, she replayed their conversation in her mind. Everything was starting to get so confusing. She walked into her classroom and sat down with a sigh. She liked Tom. He wasn't as gorgeous as Shane, but he was very good-looking. She smiled as she remembered the day they'd met at the basketball-court. He was so shy. But then, she loved Shane, didn't she?

Linda waited for Miss Caro to finish up in the painting studio. They were getting together to discuss Linda's final project. Miss Caro had said she was pleased with Linda's work lately. She was getting better at color mixtures and tonal application. Linda had shown her teacher her preliminary sketches for the painting she was thinking about doing as her final project for the class.

"I'm going to call it 'Two Lovers,' " said Linda as Miss Caro studied the sketches. "I want to try to capture on canvas that magic moment between two people when they realize they love each other."

"That's a pretty ambitious project," Miss Caro observed. "You're setting yourself quite a task. Putting a still life on canvas is one thing, but trying to get a complex emotion like love into a painting is very difficult, especially the kind of love you're talking about." She took off her glasses as she looked up at Linda. "It's almost impossible to capture romantic love in a work of art," she continued. "Maybe you should try to portray a simpler, more straightforward kind of love. There's the love between mother and daughter, for instance. That's an emotion that I'm sure you've experienced. Why don't you work with something like that instead?"

Linda felt as though Miss Caro thought she was a child without any idea about real love. But she did know, she knew she did.

"I'd really like to try it anyway," Linda persisted. "I know I can do it. Won't you at least let me give it a try?"

"Well"—she rolled a pencil in her hands for a moment—"all right. I'll approve these sketches and your project for the final. But give it some more thought. It's only the middle of the term, you have some time before finals."

"Thanks, Miss Caro," said Linda. "I really appreciate it. And I'm going to do well on the midterm tests. I just know it. Cindy and I have been studying together for weeks."

"Good. I like to see that kind of effort," Miss Caro said.

Linda left the studio and stood in the hall

staring at her drawing of Shane. As she studied the lines, she tried to decide how she'd put it on canvas—what colors and background she'd use. She was lost in thought when suddenly someone called her name. She looked up and saw Tom standing beside her.

"Hi, Linda," he said. His voice was tentative.

"Oh, hi, Tom."

Cradling his books under his arm, he looked over the top of the sketch pad she was holding. "What have you got there? Another drawing?"

Linda quickly pulled the cover of the pad down over the drawing. "Oh, they're nothing really. Just some rough sketches," she said.

"I'd like to see some of your stuff sometime. Honestly." In a teasing voice, he added, "I let you hear my songs."

Linda laughed. "Actually, I'd like to show you my work sometime. But only the stuff that's finished. I feel so self-conscious about showing things to people before I'm really happy with them. You see, I *know* what the final drawing is supposed to look like, but usually the early sketches just look like a bunch of scribbles."

Tom nodded. "I know that feeling. The same thing happens to me when I'm writing a song. I don't like to have anyone hear a song until I'm ready to perform it."

"I guess that's the same sort of thing," Linda

agreed. "When you're still in the process of creating something, it's like your own little version of the world. You don't want anyone to see it until it's just the way that you want it."

Neither of them spoke for a moment.

"Well—" Tom shuffled his feet. "I told Kim that I'm playing at the Bleecker Café again the weekend after next. I asked her to tell you, but now I can tell you myself. And I guess I just did, didn't I?"

Linda laughed. "Yes, I guess you did."

"I was kind of hoping that you guys could make it down for one of the shows. Either night. I'd really like you to be there."

"I'd like to come down," Linda said without hesitation. Then she paused. "But I'll have to check and see what's up. I'm not sure—I don't know if anything's already been planned."

"I understand," he said. "I hope you can make it."

Linda smiled. She was surprised when she heard herself say, "I hope I can, too."

"Oh, by the way," said Tom, "did you get a chance to listen to that tape I gave you a while ago?"

Linda brightened. "Yes. Yes, I did. I really liked it. I thought the first song was great. 'Love Has Its Own Kind of Time,' right?"

Tom nodded.

"It made me feel—"

"Feel what?" Tom asked eagerly.

The song reminded Linda of how she had felt about Shane that afternoon she had first heard it. She had been so confused about their relationship. In fact, she still was. But how could she tell Tom about that?

"I felt as though someone were talking to me," she finally said. "Not to *me* exactly, but you know, it was as if somebody were telling me about something he understood very well—and really meant every word that he said."

"Remember what I told you before?" asked Tom. "You can't write a good song unless you feel it inside? The same thing goes for any work of art, but I guess you know that."

Linda did feel the same way. And she began to feel something else, too. It was as if she were seeing Tom for the first time. She had always known that he was a good writer and musician. But this was something else—something more.

"You know, I really respect that honesty in your music," Linda said.

"I'm glad," he said, smiling.

"Well, I've got to get going," said Linda. "I've got another class in a few minutes, and somehow I always manage to be late. I've really got to run."

"OK," Tom said. "But don't forget about the

weekend after next. I'll be at the café both Friday and Saturday nights. I hope I'll see you there."

"I'll try," said Linda, yelling as she ran down the hall toward her classroom. "I'll really try to be there."

As she arrived at the open classroom door near the end of the corridor, she turned around, and looked back down the hall. Tom was still there, watching her.

They smiled at each other. Then she disappeared into the room.

She quickly took her seat under Mr. Cates's disapproving stare. As soon as she was seated, he launched into the day's lesson.

Cindy was sitting next to Linda, and she giggled softly under her breath when Linda arrived.

"You never make this class on time," she whispered. "If you don't watch out Cates is going to make you write a paper on getting to English class before the bell." Linda stifled a smile as she opened her copy of *The Catcher in the Rye.*

As the class progressed, Linda's mind wandered. She wondered what Shane was doing just then. What was he thinking? What was he wearing? Should she call him again? It was getting harder and harder to wait.

Then Linda started thinking about Tom. It

was as though she had met another person when she had last seen him. But was he really that much different, or was it just that she had never bothered to discover what he was like? She had been so wrapped up in Shane that she hadn't really bothered to listen to Tom—to try to get to know him.

When she was with Shane, all she could think about was how much she cared about him. The world stood at a distance, so far away that it almost seemed as though it weren't there at all. Thoughts like the ones she was having then about Tom would have never entered her mind if Shane had been there. When she was with Shane he was the most important person in the world.

But she felt that way only when they were together, and that wasn't often enough. And she couldn't keep calling him. It just wouldn't be right. If only that special feeling could last through the times they were apart.

"Linda, I would like you to explain the outline of this story to the class. You *do* know which story we were reading, don't you, Linda?"

It was Mr. Cates.

"Are you with us today, Linda?" Mr. Cates asked sarcastically. "You seem like a bright enough young lady. I'm sure the rest of the class would be delighted to have you join them."

A murmur of laughter swept through the

room. Linda's face began to turn bright crimson as Mr. Cates leaned down over her desk.

"I'm waiting, Linda," he said in his stiff manner. "Do you think you might join us today?"

Linda stammered, "I—I'm sorry, Mr. Cates. I was just—I was—it won't happen again."

"Thank you, Miss Wills," he said formally. "Now, where were we?"

The class continued, and Linda heard Cindy giggle. She turned toward her friend and gave her a withering stare. But Cindy just continued to chuckle.

After class, Linda started laughing, too, as she thought about her teacher's angry face. The two of them walked down the corridor making fun of Mr. Cates's mannerisms. As they turned the corner, they ran into Kim and Kristen, who were headed to their next class.

Linda greeted them and looked apprehensively at Kristen, who smiled briefly. Oddly, Linda felt a little more sure of herself in front of Kristen because Cindy was there.

Cindy told Kim and Kristen about the scene in their English class. Kim laughed along with Linda at it. The story even drew a muted laugh from Kristen.

"You'd better get your head out of the clouds, Linda," said Kim with a smile. "I had Cates last year, and he can get pretty tough at exam time."

"I'll be careful," Linda promised.

Linda turned to Kristen. "I'd still like to get together with you one of these days and compare sketches," she said, a little amazed at her own forthrightness.

Kristen looked down at the books in her arms and then back at Linda. "Sure. One of these days. Maybe after midterms. Things are a little busy right now."

"Well, we have to get to class," Kim said. She waved to Linda and Cindy as she turned down the hall. Kristen turned with her, raising her hand in a small wave as she went.

Cindy and Linda went off down the corridor. "Kristen's nice, but she can be kind of strange," Cindy said.

"I know," Linda replied. "But at least she talked to me this time. I guess Kim was right when she said that you just have to give her time to open up."

"Well, anyway, I have to get to gym," said Cindy. "I'll see you later. Don't forget about getting together with me to study for midterms."

"I won't," said Linda.

Cindy broke into a run. Linda climbed a short flight of stairs that led to the cafeteria where she wanted to get a snack. As she stood on the top step, she could see across the large dining room to the steps on the far side of the cafeteria. She spotted Shane. He was just leaving the room, and there was a girl on either side of him. Linda didn't recognize them, but Shane was talking to them, and they were smiling at him. Then they disappeared down the stairs leading to the other side of the hall.

Linda stood still. A girl bumped into her as she walked by. "Excuse me," Linda said automatically. She walked into the cafeteria, put her books down on the table and eased herself into a chair.

So what, she thought. *I'm not the only girl that Shane knows. I'm not the only person he talks to. He has a life of his own. And I'm part of that life. A big part.* She noticed her heart was beating harder. *It doesn't mean a thing*, she reminded herself firmly.

Chapter Thirteen

As midterms were approaching, studying took up more and more of Linda's time. And the teachers weren't giving any breaks, either. They seemed to increase the nightly workloads and assignments. Linda kept reminding herself that the discipline necessary to get all of it done would help her in life. Artists had to be disciplined.

That Thursday Kim and Linda were riding the train home from school when Kim mentioned that Tom was playing at the café the following weekend. Linda said that she knew.

"You saw Tom?" Kim asked. Linda nodded. "When?"

"Yesterday afternoon. We met in the hallway at school. I was on my way to Mr. Cates's English class, and I was late again."

"What did you guys talk about?" Kim asked, sounding curious.

"There wasn't a whole lot to say, really. We talked about art and found out that we think a lot alike."

"Tom's a nice guy," said Kim.

"Yes, he is," Linda agreed. "But I get the feeling that you're trying to get us together."

"It's not that, Linda. It's just that I think—well, you know, you've been kind of hung up on Shane lately."

"What does that have to do with anything? Besides, I'm not 'hung up' on Shane. We see each other, that's all." She didn't mention seeing Shane in the cafeteria the day before.

"You make it sound so casual," Kim said.

"It isn't casual. It's—it's—" Linda turned away.

Kim put her hand on Linda's shoulder. "When was the last time he called you?" she asked gently.

Linda leaned her head back against the top of the plastic subway car seat and sighed. "Not since that night we went to the movies. Six days and twenty-one and a half hours ago."

"You're keeping a count like that?" said Kim. "Isn't that a little silly?"

"There's nothing silly about this at all," Linda snapped. Then she leaned her head back again. "Oh, Kim, I don't know what to think anymore.

I'm so confused. When I'm with him I don't have a care in the world. But when I'm not, all I do is think about him."

"I know the feeling," Kim said sympathetically. "This kind of thing happens to everybody at one time or another." Then she paused and asked, "Do you know whether he's seeing other girls?"

The thought had never entered Linda's mind. Sure, there had been girls in Shane's dressing room that first night, but that was to be expected. Shane was popular. And besides, Linda had only met him that night.

"No, he never said anything about other girls," Linda said. "And I never asked him. It's not the kind of thing I ask. But I know he isn't seeing anyone else; he wouldn't do that to me. Shane's not that kind of person."

Kim dropped the subject, and they talked about school for the rest of the ride.

When they got home Kim's mother wasn't there; she was still at work. Linda went to the kitchen to get a snack, and Kim went into the living room. She turned on the answering machine to see if anyone had called.

The first message was from Kim's boss, Heather. Kim listened as Heather explained that the other salesgirl was going to be leaving in about three weeks. She said that if Linda was interested in the job she should call by Saturday.

"Linda! Linda, guess what?" Kim shouted across the apartment. "The job's open. Heather wants you to call her!"

Linda let out a whoop of happiness. "That's great. No more penny pinching," she cheered. "*And* no more borrowing your clothes all the time. Now I can buy my own."

"It's not definite," Kim reminded her. "But I know you're going to get it. Just think, we'll be working together."

The two girls hugged each other and jumped up and down. Then Linda went back into the kitchen, humming a song as she stared into the refrigerator. Kim went back to checking the rest of the messages. The next one was from Kim's mother, reminding her to pick up some things at the store for supper. There was a long beep after she hung up. Then, even though she was in the next room, Linda could hear Shane's voice on the machine.

"Linda, it's Shane," he said. "I was wondering if you'd be interested in going out tomorrow night. I've got two tickets to the Journey concert at Madison Square Garden. Please call me as soon as you can to let me know. Sorry for the short notice, but it was the best I could do. Talk to you later. Bye."

Linda shouted again. "Two pieces of great news, one right after the other. This is great." She put her hands on Kim's shoulders and squeezed them. "See, I knew he'd call. I knew it. He was probably just really busy in the studio, that's all. I'll bet that someone at Journey's record company gave him the tickets and that as soon as he got them, he called me. That's why it's such short notice."

Linda was thrilled, and Kim seemed happy for her. Linda went to the phone immediately to call Shane. She dialed the number, and it rang a few times, then she heard the receiver being picked up. It was Shane.

"Hi, Shane. It's Linda."

"Oh, hi, Linda. How are you doing? Did you get my message?"

"I sure did. Oh, Shane, I'd love to go."

"Great!" He sounded glad that she'd said yes. "I can't wait to see you."

"Me, either," Linda replied in a happy voice.

Shane asked her to meet him at the Garden since he'd be working in the studio right up until showtime. "I might be a little late, so don't worry if you're a couple of minutes late, too. Maybe we'll even walk in during the first act. That would be real hip."

"All right, Shane," said Linda. "I'll meet you

at seven-thirty out in front of the Garden. What should I wear?"

"Wear something really rock 'n' roll. With that beautiful blond hair of yours you always look good in black. But whatever you wear, I'm sure you'll look fine."

"OK. See you then," said Linda.

"Yes, see you tomorrow." He hung up the phone.

"Well?" Kim, who had been waiting nearby, asked. "What's up? Are you going?"

"Yes. Tomorrow night. It's going to be so great! I really like Journey. I'd like to see the band that's opening for them, too, but Shane says it's cooler to be late. I guess that way everybody sees you walking in."

"Not that anyone knows who he is," said Kim.

"*I* know who he is," said Linda. "And that's all that's important."

"Well, you'd better start cracking those books if you want to go out tomorrow night," Kim said.

"Oh, gosh," Linda exclaimed. "I'm going to have to cancel on Cindy again. We were supposed to study together over the weekend. I hope she'll understand. We can salvage one day on the books, anyway."

"That's what friends are for, right? To understand," Kim said.

Linda smiled. "That's right—friend." She ran into her room with her book bag. Within minutes, she was back. She ran over to Kim and said, a little sheepishly, "Even if I get the job, work won't start for a couple of weeks yet, so—"

"So?" Kim said with a smile.

"Can I borrow those shoes again?"

Kim laughed. "Sure. The shoes *and* the scarf."

Chapter Fourteen

On Friday night the temperature had dropped to the thirties. A strong, cold wind blew from one side of the city to the other. And there was even a hint of frost on the windows of the apartment as Linda rushed around getting ready for the concert.

Kim did her best to help Linda with her makeup.

"Hold still, dummy, or I'll never get this right," she complained as she brushed Linda's eyelids with shadow.

Linda's mind was in a whirl. There was no reason for it, but she had the feeling that that night was going to be special—more than just another date.

At seven o'clock, Linda was ready. Her aunt

Catherine gave her a ten-dollar bill in case she needed extra money. Linda thanked her and gave her a kiss as she flew out the door and down to the lobby. Marley waved to Linda, but she ran out and flagged down her own cab. "Eighth Avenue and Thirty-fourth Street, please," she told the driver.

"Going to that Journey concert tonight?" he asked.

"Yes," Linda said, a little astonished. "How did you know that?"

"I'm a big Journey fan myself. If I didn't have to drive tonight, I'd probably be going, too."

Linda and the cab driver talked about music on the way down to Madison Square Garden. Their conversation took her mind off her nervousness, and Linda was glad. Within a few minutes, though, they hit traffic going downtown on Seventh Avenue, and the driver concentrated on weaving in and out of the mass of cars, trucks, and buses. Linda was left to her thoughts.

What will tonight be like? she wondered. *Maybe I shouldn't worry about things so much,* she thought. *I should just let whatever happens happen.*

But let it be great! she thought with a smile.

She sat back in the seat for the rest of the

ride. The taxi pulled up in front of Madison Square Garden a few minutes later. The meter read six dollars and ten cents. Linda gave the driver seven dollars and said goodbye to him. He wished her luck and told her to enjoy the concert.

There was a huge crowd in line, and that worried Linda. How was she ever going to find Shane in that mob, she wondered? He had told her to meet him in front of the ticket windows, but it looked like every Journey fan in New York was there.

It was seven twenty-five; she was a little early. She stood huddled in her jacket, trying to stay warm as the wind whipped around her from all directions. The large plaza in front of the arena offered no protection from the cold.

Fifteen minutes went by. Then twenty. Shane had said he might be late, but twenty minutes? The crowds had moved through the gates, leaving just Linda and some ticket scalpers in the almost deserted plaza.

After another ten minutes Linda decided to call home to see if there had been any word from Shane. As she looked around for a phone booth, she saw a man walking casually into the plaza area. His head was bent down into his coat, but there was something familiar about the way that he walked. He came closer, and Linda realized it was Tom. He looked up, saw Linda standing there shivering, and hurried over to her.

"What are you doing out here?" Tom asked.

Linda's teeth chattered as she spoke. "I'm—I'm waiting for someone. I was supposed to meet him here. What are *you* doing here?"

"I've got tickets to the show. I'm late because I got stuck in a computer class. But look, Linda—uh, my friend who I bought the ticket for got sick and said I should give it to someone else. But no one could make it on such short notice. I'd be glad to give you the ticket if you want. We could see the show together."

Linda wondered what she should do. She was freezing, and Shane was later than she had ever thought he would be. But if she left then and he came, she'd feel terrible.

Linda stood there, frozen by the cold and her indecision. Just then, another person approached them. It was Shane.

"Hi, Linda. Sorry I'm late. The session ran real late, and it was tough getting down here. I'm really sorry."

He took her hand in his. "Ooh, it's cold. Let's go inside."

"It's OK, Shane. I understand." She didn't really, but what could she say? Then she remembered Tom. "Shane, you know Tom Hagen, don't you? He's going to the show, too."

Shane looked over at Tom. "Yeah, I know Tom. Hi, how are you doing?" Before Tom could reply, Shane continued. "I've got two seats in the press area right up front. Let's go." He took Linda's other hand, and they walked toward the gates. As he left, he looked back at Tom and said, "See you around."

Linda turned and tried to say goodbye to Tom as Shane pulled her to the gate. The wind came up and muffled her words, but she saw Tom wave. He looked so forlorn standing there, all alone, and she felt bad about what had just happened.

Inside, the arena was warm and noisy. It felt good to be out of the cold. As they took their seats in the fifth row, Linda noticed they were surrounded by music reporters. She could tell who they were from their laminated plastic identification tags. There wasn't much chance to talk because the opening band was very loud. But pretty soon Linda got caught up in the excitement of the performance.

The band ended its show fifteen minutes later. In between the two acts, the sound system played tapes, and the volume was a bit more reasonable.

"I was really getting worried out there," Linda

said to Shane. "I thought you might not make it."

"I said I was sorry, Linda," said Shane. "There was nothing I could do about it. I had to be there to do some more guitar parts on the tape. All that matters is that I'm here now, right?"

Linda nodded. She was about to say something about Tom when Shane added, "Here with you, that is."

Shane reached into his coat pocket and pulled out a cassette player and a tape. As he put the tape into the player, he said, "This is a rough mix of a new song we're doing. Why don't you listen to it while I talk to some of these people?"

Linda took the headphones and placed them over her head. "Is 'Artist' on the tape?" she asked.

"No," Shane replied, "but I think you'll like this one." Linda pushed the play button, and the tape began to roll. Shane's voice came up loud and strong over the guitars.

She sat back and listened, watching Shane as he talked with some of the people seated around them. He seemed to know some of them, and—what was more—they seemed to know who he was, too. That impressed Linda. Shane was obviously close to making it.

She held the headphones close to her ears to

block out the arena's sound system. The song was called "Who's Gonna Love You?" There was a hard, tough edge to the song. The lyrics were about a guy who says he doesn't care anymore about the person he once said he loved; he says he's glad he's free again because now he can find a girl who will be what he wants her to be.

The song exploded into a guitar solo that Linda knew had to be Shane. She could almost picture him as he stood there in the studio, his fingers flying over the guitar neck, a lock of blond hair falling over his forehead.

But as she listened to the lyrics again, she felt that there was something unsettling about the song. She wondered if it represented a side of Shane that she had not seen before, or if he'd just made the song up. Shane did have a very strong personality, but the thoughts he had expressed in the song left Linda wondering what had prompted him to write it.

As Linda took the headphones off to ask Shane about the song, the lights went down and the Journey show began. The lights and the outfits were dazzling, and Linda was soon swept away by them. It was the first really big concert she had ever been to. There was a large arena back in Kansas City, but she had never gotten the chance to see a show there. And even that was nothing like the Garden. The place was so huge.

Journey played song after song that she knew, and Linda sang along with most of them. But about halfway through the concert, she found herself wondering where Tom was sitting. She wondered how he felt, sitting all alone. It was nice of him to have offered his ticket to her like that. He had paid for them. Shane had gotten these passes for free. Not that that made a difference, but still, she thought about it.

After Journey had finished their third encore, the show ended. Shane turned to Linda. "A friend of mine says he can get passes to go backstage and meet the band. Would you like that?"

"Would I ever!" she exclaimed. She followed Shane and a man with long hair as they waded through the crowd. They came to a burly security guard at the stage entrance, and he inspected the man's pass. He listened as the man explained that Shane and Linda were his guests. The guard nodded to Linda and Shane as he let the three of them through.

The backstage area was a mass of people. Most of them were moving equipment and rushing back and forth. Linda held Shane's hand tightly. They finally made it to a set of doors that led to the band's private rooms. They stopped again for Shane's friend to explain the situation. Then he turned and said something to Shane. Shane nodded as he spoke, then he looked at Linda. "Look, I'm afraid there's a little problem. The band doesn't want too many people in the dressing room at a time, so my friend says that only he and I can go in. You don't mind, do you? I mean, it could be very useful for me to meet these guys. It could mean a lot later on down the line."

Linda hesitated for a second. "OK, Shane," she said. "I know it's important to you. But, please, don't leave me out here too long. I don't know anybody."

"Great. I'll be right back," Shane said as he turned and went into the room with his friend. Linda looked around as she waited. Men ran around lugging huge pieces of equipment, like guitar amplifiers and speaker cabinets. They yelled at one another from across the wide backstage area, directing the equipment onto trucks. As she waited, several other people went through the doors up to the dressing room, some with cameras strapped around their shoulders. When the door was opened, Linda could see Shane standing with his arm around someone as a photographer took their picture. She wished she could be in there with him.

She waited for about twenty minutes altogether. Then Shane came out and took her by the hand. "Linda, I've been invited to a party the band is throwing back at the hotel," he explained. "Would you like to come along?"

"It's kind of late, Shane," she said. "I've got to be back home by eleven-thirty."

"Well, I really want to go to this party," he said. "I've already met a lot of important people here, and I'm sure I'll meet more up there later."

"But what about me?" she asked. "Don't you think I'm important, too?"

Shane's blue eyes softened. "Of course you are, Linda. You're very important to me." He took her by the arm and drew her close to him. "But you have to understand. This is an important move in my career. It could open many new doors for me. You know how hard I've been working to get this far."

Linda felt confused, but she knew that this must be important to Shane. "What should I do? I've got to get home in a half hour—an hour at the absolute most."

"Look, the only thing you can do is go get a cab out front. Don't worry about a thing. I'll call you tomorrow." Then he wrapped his arms around her and kissed her. He brought his face close to her ear and in a breathy voice said, "I love you, Linda."

She smiled. "I love you, too, Shane." They

kissed once more, and then Shane went back into the dressing room again.

Linda turned and made her way to the doors that led to the street. *He finally said it!* she thought to herself. It made her feel so good. But she wished that Shane didn't have to go to that party. She wished that he could be with her now, holding her hand and saying that he loved her over and over again. But something was bothering Linda. *If he loves me, why am I alone now?* she wondered. Shane could have at least taken her home, and then gone on to the party.

When she reached the street, it was almost deserted. The wind howled fiercely as she stood in front of Madison Square Garden trying to find a cab. She pulled Kim's scarf tightly around her neck, but it wasn't exactly designed for warmth. Taxis with couples in the back rolled up Eighth Avenue, passing Linda as she stood on the curb. Finally, she saw an empty one. He pulled over when he saw Linda's outstretched arm. She got in and told the driver where she wanted to go.

The cab moved back into traffic and turned east. Linda tried to sort out her feelings. She had waited so long to hear Shane say he loved her. But as she sat in the cab all alone, an ache of disappointment rose in her throat. *He loves me, he has to love me,* she thought over and over. But the more she said it, the more it sounded as though she were trying to convince herself. She looked at her reflection in the window of the cab as it sped uptown. A tear rolled down her cheek. She remembered that the last time she'd been in a cab, she also cried. And she had been alone then, too.

Chapter Fifteen

Saturday seemed to drag by. Linda opened a book to study, only to close it minutes later. She constantly looked over at the phone as if staring at it would make it ring. Kim was filling in for a friend at work, so Linda was alone. Her cousin had left her a note on her bed since she had gone to sleep before Linda had gotten back from the concert. "Heather said to tell you that you definitely have the job," the note on Kim's personal stationery read. "You start right after school on November fifteenth. Heather also said she's glad you'll be working with us. You must have made a great impression on her when you called yesterday. Hope you had a good time at the show with Shane. Talk to you when I get home. Love, K."

Thick, gray clouds hung over the city that afternoon, threatening to either rain or snow. It didn't help Linda's spirits at all to look out of the window at the dark sky.

She took her math book back into the living room and sat down on the couch with a pencil and some graph paper. Then the phone rang, and Linda literally leaped to answer it. "Hello," she said before she even had the receiver to her mouth.

"Linda? Is that you? It's Cindy."

"Oh, hi, Cindy," said Linda, trying to hide the disappointment in her voice. "How are you?"

"I'm fine, Linda, but I've got a problem about tonight," she said. "I'm not going to be able to get together with you to study."

"Why? What's up?" Linda asked.

"Well—I, uh, I have to go visit my uncle," she said. "He's sick."

Linda sat down on the edge of the sofa. "Oh, Cindy, I'm sorry. What's wrong with him?"

"He's got, well, he's sort of got this very bad flulike thing that's going around," said Cindy. "He's got it bad, and my mom asked me to go over there and help him. You know, do some grocery shopping for him, that sort of thing."

"Be careful you don't catch it. Take some vitamin C." Linda closed the book in front of her.

"Where does your uncle live? Is it in the city?" she asked.

"Well, sort of," said Cindy. "He's over in Brooklyn, near where we used to live. I'll be gone all day, and I probably won't be back until sometime on Sunday. I'm just about to leave. It's a long ride."

"OK," Linda said, "but we'd better try to get together pretty soon. The art midterm is next Thursday. That's what we really need to do most of the work on."

"Right," said Cindy. "Don't worry. We'll do it. I promise."

"Now you sound like me," said Linda, smiling for the first time all day. "You're not just making this up to get back at me for all the times I did this to you, are you?"

"Of course not," Cindy said. "Look, Linda, I have to run now. I have to get ready. You know, to go over to Brooklyn."

"OK," said Linda. "I'll see you in a couple of days. Maybe you can call me when you get back, and we can set up a time to get together."

"Right. I'll call you when I get back," said Cindy. "Bye."

Linda hung up the phone feeling depressed. Everything else was going wrong, why not this, too? But she wondered why Cindy hadn't at least asked her about how the concert had been.

Or about Shane. She would have liked to have had someone to talk to about it. Kim wasn't around, and her aunt Catherine was out with a client. But then, her cousin had always seemed a little critical of Shane, and her aunt probably wouldn't have understood anyway. It was probably better that she was alone.

Linda walked over to the window and gazed out at the thickening clouds. *Something's wrong,* she thought. *Very wrong. Shane said he loved me, but then why did he make me go home alone last night? And why hasn't he called me?* The same questions she had asked herself the night before now went around and around in her mind. *Would Shane have said he loved me just to string me along? Was he the kind of guy who would do that sort of thing? How do I know? How will I know?*

Linda went back to the couch and picked up her math book again. The hours passed, and the phone remained silent.

Her aunt came home about five that evening. She made a comment about the terrible weather, and Linda said that she hadn't been out all day. "It's just as well," her aunt said. "It's pretty raw out there, and I think it's going to get worse." She smiled at Linda. "Isn't that what they always say—it gets worse before it gets better?"

Linda tried to return her smile. Her aunt went into the kitchen to prepare dinner. Kim came in a little while after that, looking pale and tired.

"What's the matter, Kim?" her mother asked. "Did you have a bad day at the shop?"

"I don't feel very well," Kim said in a weak voice. "My head hurts, and I feel kind of achy."

Her mother put her hand against Kim's forehead. "I think you've got a fever. Go get into bed, and I'll bring a thermometer in."

As it turned out, Kim had a temperature of 101 degrees. Her mother made her some soup, and Linda went in to keep her company while she ate. "Well, that's one way of getting out of midterms," she said, trying to cheer up her cousin.

Kim tried to laugh, but it hurt her throat. "The way I feel right now, I think I'd rather face a math final."

"I hope you feel better soon," Linda said before closing the door. "Try to get some rest."

Linda felt pretty tired, too. She went to bed early and slept late on Sunday morning. When she went to the window of her room, she saw that the weather hadn't improved much. The clouds still hung in the sky, looking mean and threatening. She spent the rest of the weekend studying as well as she could. Thoughts of Shane competed with algebra equations and history dates. She tried her best to concentrate.

Kim's cold lingered, and she stayed in bed. She was still there on Monday morning as Linda left for school. Linda felt strange going without Kim. She felt even more alone. Shane hadn't called, and Linda was beginning to think he wouldn't. Cindy hadn't phoned, either. Perhaps her uncle had been sicker than she had thought. Linda figured Cindy would tell her at school what had happened.

But Cindy wasn't at school. When art class was over, Linda was picking up her art materials when Miss Caro stopped her. "How's the painting coming along?"

"I haven't worked on it for a while," Linda admitted. "I guess I haven't really been inspired. It looks good so far, though. I just need to decide exactly what I want to do with it before I go any further."

"Don't worry about it too much, Linda," Miss Caro said. "It's not due till the end of the semester, so you've still got plenty of time. And it's sometimes good to step away from something that you're so involved in. A little distance will give you a new perspective on it. Sometimes you can come back and see things that you didn't see before."

149

"I guess so," Linda said. "I'll keep that in mind."

In line for lunch Linda found that nothing looked especially appetizing. Finally she picked up and paid for a salad and a container of juice, then turned around to find a place to sit. Since Cindy was out, it looked as though Linda would have to eat alone. She walked around one of the thick, round columns that ran all the way up to the cafeteria's ceiling and scanned the room looking for an empty seat. There were none. Then a hand touched her lightly on the back. "There's a place for you here," a voice said. Linda turned around. It was Kristen.

Chapter Sixteen

Linda was pleased, although a little surprised, that Kristen was so friendly. Maybe they could become friends after all, Linda thought hopefully. She sat down beside Kristen and said with a smile, "Thanks. I was beginning to think I'd have to eat standing up."

"You're welcome." Somehow, Kristen looked less severe than she usually did. Perhaps it was the muted light from the window that softened her features. "How have you been?" Kristen asked as she picked at the salad on her plate.

"I've been OK," Linda replied. "I'm glad we're sitting together. Ever since I met you, I've been hoping that we could get together sometime and talk about art. I really like your work."

"I know. I mean, I know you wanted to talk," she said. "So do I—but about something else."

"What?"

"Shane."

Linda remembered what Kim had told her that first night at Pat's—Kristen had once dated Shane. Could Kristen still be interested in him? Was he still interested in her?

"Shane's fine," Linda said in a wary tone. "Why do you want to talk about him?"

Kristen pushed her lunch away from her and put her arms on the table, leaning forward as she spoke. "I want to tell you some things you don't know about Shane," she said. "Things you need to know."

"What can you tell me?" Linda asked. "I know all—"

"No, you don't," said Kristen more forcefully. "That's why I need to talk to you. Listen, Shane and I went out together once, so I know what I'm talking about. Things didn't end nicely."

"Do you still want to go out with him?" Linda asked hesitantly.

Kristen's smile was tight. "Oh, no way. No, I'm not the least bit interested in Shane anymore." She looked over at the windows and at the gray clouds that covered the sky. "Not anymore."

She turned back to face Linda. "Shane really had me wrapped around his finger at one time. He really did." She sighed. "I thought the two of us were going to last forever. There's something about him that's irresistible—a sensitivity that strikes you from the very beginning."

"I know that," Linda said. "I mean, I feel the same way."

"That's just the problem," Kristen explained. "All the girls see that in him."

Linda didn't like the direction in which the conversation was heading. What was Kristen trying to do, break them up? Why?

"I can't stop you from going out with Shane. But I have to be sure you know what he's really like." Kristen leaned even closer to Linda. "Shane's going to hurt you, Linda. No matter what you think now, no matter how good things seem to be, he's going to hurt you in the end."

"No," Linda argued. "I'm not sure why you're saying these things, but I know they're not true. Shane wouldn't hurt me. He loves me. He told me so!" She was beginning to get angry.

"That doesn't surprise me," Kristen replied. "He told me the same thing. I remember how sincere he sounded. I really believed him. I *wanted* to believe him."

"Why should I believe you?" Linda snapped. "Why should I believe you and not Shane?"

"Because—" Kristen stopped. She looked up at the ceiling, then back at Linda. "Because I don't want you to get hurt. Believe it or not, I like you, Linda.

"When I saw you and Shane that first night, I saw what was going on, and I knew what was going to happen. I was furious, but I was also afraid to say anything. If I had, everyone would have thought I was just jealous. After all, everyone knows how crazy I was about Shane. And besides, you would never have believed me anyway.

"It was terrible, Linda. I couldn't even talk with Kim about how I felt. And Kim and I talk about everything. Then I realized that the one person I could talk to—the person I *should* talk to—was you."

Linda listened. She wanted to defend Shane, but she couldn't. She thought of all the times Shane had let her down, all the times he had forgotten to call her or called her at the last minute. Linda remembered her disappointment when Shane hadn't taken her home after the Journey concert.

"I know that Shane means a lot to you now," Kristen continued urgently. "But he's not for real. The only person that Shane really cares about is Shane. That's what's going to keep him from ever loving anyone. That's also what's going to prevent him from ever being a really successful musician."

"But what about the song he wrote for me?" Linda asked, clinging to her last bit of hope.

"You probably didn't hear it, but it's called 'Artist,' and I inspired Shane to write it. He wouldn't have written that song if he hadn't loved me."

"I know all about that song," Kristen said. "I know it very well." Kristen then hummed a few notes and gently sang a line from the chorus. "I know that song," she continued, "because Shane said he wrote it for me."

Linda wanted to deny that what Kristen had said was true. She wanted to argue, but in her heart she knew Kristen was right. She guessed she had known it for a long time but just hadn't been willing to admit it to herself.

Kristen stood up. "I have to go now, Linda. I have a class to get to. I'm sorry, but I had to tell you." Then she leaned down and said, "I hope we can be friends from now on."

Linda looked up at her. "I don't know what's going to happen, Kristen. I guess I have a lot of thinking to do. But I think—I think, we can be friends." She smiled, and Kristen smiled back.

Chapter Seventeen

Linda was still in a daze as she walked from the cafeteria to her next class. In a funny way, she felt relieved. Now she knew exactly where she stood with Shane—nowhere. There would be no more wondering when he'd call or whether she'd see him. She wouldn't feel as if she had to wait to make plans until she knew whether he was going to have time to see her.

Suddenly Linda thought of Tom—kind, sweet Tom. He was playing at the Bleecker Café that weekend, and just then Linda wanted very badly to be there for the show. She decided to call him when she got home that afternoon. But before she did she had to speak to Shane. There was no reason not to call him now—not after what Kristen had told her.

Linda walked into Mr. Cates's English class, realizing that she was early for the very first time. The room was almost empty, but as she looked around, she saw Cindy sitting at her desk.

"I thought you were out sick today," she said, walking over to where her friend was sitting. "I thought you'd caught whatever your uncle had."

Cindy looked troubled. "Linda, we have a few minutes before class starts, and I need to talk to you. Can we go out into the hall?"

They walked out of the classroom and over to the drinking fountain, which was set back in a little niche in the hall. "Linda, I didn't go to Brooklyn this weekend," Cindy began. "I don't have an uncle there, either."

"What? Where *were* you?"

Cindy looked at the floor for a moment, composing her thoughts. "I don't know how to tell you this—" she started. "Oh, Linda, Shane called me on Saturday. He asked me out." Cindy's voice was trembling slightly. "He asked me to go to a movie with him that night. He told me—he told me it was OK with you, that you two weren't going steady or anything. I knew it didn't sound right, not after what you had told me about how you felt about him."

She pushed the button on the water fountain, and took a drink of water. "I said yes. I know I shouldn't have, but— Oh, Linda, I'm so sorry. I was on my way to meet him and just before I got on the subway, I stopped. I realized then that it *wasn't* right—that I'd be hurting you if I went out with him. I just couldn't do it—not to a friend like you."

Cindy was on the verge of tears, and Linda reached out and put her arm on her friend's shoulder to comfort her.

"I couldn't face you this morning," Cindy continued. "That's why I wasn't in homeroom or art class. That's why I made up that story. I knew I should have turned Shane down right from the beginning, but when I didn't, I was too scared to face you knowing what I'd done."

"It's OK, Cindy," Linda said in a gentle voice. "I understand, really. Thanks for telling me. I know it must have been hard."

Just then, Mr. Cates came by. "Is there anything wrong here?"

"No, Mr. Cates," Linda replied. "It's nothing, really. We'll be there in a minute."

Mr. Cates frowned and walked into the classroom. Cindy composed herself as well as she could, then followed Linda into English class.

Linda had to struggle through the rest of school that day, alternating between feelings of hurt and anger. On the subway ride home, she was so lost in her own thoughts that she nearly missed her connecting train. Then she got off at the wrong stop. She came out of the subway at Seventy-seventh Street and had to walk back to Seventy-second. Nodding glumly at Marley when she got to her building, she walked through the lobby to the elevators.

When she went into the apartment, she saw Kim lying under a blanket on the couch, reading a book. Kim looked up at her. "Hi. How was school?"

Linda walked over to the couch and put her book bag down. Then, with a heavy sigh, she told Kim the whole story.

"That creep!" Kim said when Linda was finished. "I don't believe it. And to hit on your best friend, too."

Linda looked at Kim seriously. "I don't know what to do," she said. Her resolve of earlier in the day was fading fast. "I wish I could just go to sleep and wake up tomorrow to find out that this whole thing was a bad dream."

"I know what you mean," Kim said sympathetically. "But you're going to have to face it."

"I know," Linda agreed. "And I think the thing that's bothering me the most is the way I treated Tom. I literally ignored the poor guy. Shane had me so mixed up that I couldn't see what Tom was trying to say. So, I decided to call him this afternoon. But now I'm wondering if I should."

"You definitely should," said Kim with a twinkle in her eye. "He called you a little while ago. He wants you to call him back."

"What should I say?" Linda asked, suddenly panic-stricken.

Kim smiled. "I wouldn't worry about that. I think you'll know what to say."

Linda went over to the phone and dialed the number Kim had copied down. Tom answered on the second ring.

"Tom? Hi, it's Linda. Kim said you called. I don't know what— "

"Hi, Linda. Listen, I was just calling to remind you that I'm playing at the Bleecker Café over the weekend. And"—he hesitated—"look, I also wanted to say something else. I know that you're seeing Shane, and I know that you really care about him. But I want you to know that I care about you, too. I haven't known how to come out and tell you that, but it's gotten to the point where I had to say something. I just want a chance—just a chance."

Linda was surprised, but she was smiling, too. She wished he had said something a long time ago. Maybe that would have changed everything. But then she wondered if she would have listened. Maybe he had been trying to say it all along?

"Tom," Linda said, "don't worry. I'll be at your show. I'll be there both nights if you want me to come. And, Tom—I'm sorry."

There was a pause on the other end of the line. "Sorry for what?"

"Sorry for not listening. Or maybe, for not being able to listen."

She hung up the phone and went back to the couch where Kim was.

"Well, what happened?" Kim asked.

"I'm going down to the café to see Tom on Friday. Maybe on Saturday, too."

"What about Shane? Aren't you going to do anything about him? Especially after what he did to you."

"I'll deal with Shane," Linda said in a firm tone. She had planned to call him, but another idea was forming in her head. A perfect idea.

Chapter Eighteen

The rest of the week went by in a flash. Linda tried to clear her mind of everything but work as she studied, but it wasn't easy. Thoughts about Shane would come creeping into her mind, despite her efforts. And even though they always made her angry, she knew that the worst was over. And now she had Tom. Knowing that he was on her side made the terrible way Shane had treated her seem less important.

Finally Friday came. "I'm going home to collapse," Cindy said as they walked to the subway. "I'm so glad that this week is over."

"Me, too," Linda said. "In more ways than one."

When she got home, Linda stretched out on her bed. She just wanted to relax for a while.

After all, she had a big night ahead of her. When they had finished dinner, Linda went into her room immediately to start getting ready. Kim walked into Linda's room a few minutes later.

"Everybody's going to see Shane at Pat's tonight," Kim said. "But we can meet you over at the café for Tom's show later."

"No, I'll be at Pat's tonight, too," Linda replied.

"You're going to come with us to Pat's?" Kim asked, her voice full of surprise.

"That's right."

"I don't understand. Why?"

"Don't worry," Linda answered. "For the first time, I know exactly what I'm doing as far as Shane is concerned."

"OK," Kim said doubtfully. They busied themselves getting ready. Kim rushed around as usual, but Linda took her time. She carefully put on her makeup and got dressed, making sure she looked her best.

They went down to the lobby together, and Marley called a cab for them. The two girls were silent all the way downtown.

The cab pulled up in front of Pat's. As they walked down the short flight of stairs that led into the club, Linda and Kim spotted Amy, Paul, Tammy, and Jerry sitting at a large, round table. They went over to where their friends were sitting, and everyone started talking at once. Because of midterms and studying, no one had really had time to get together and chat.

The waitress came over, and they ordered a couple of pitchers of soda. Just as the waitress returned with their order, Linda saw Shane step out of the dressing room. She also saw a girl walk out behind him, and Linda watched him make his way across the room.

"We just finished the tape yesterday," Shane announced to everyone when he got to the table. "It sounds incredible. I think we're really going to make it this time."

Then he leaned down to give Linda a kiss on the cheek. "Hi, there. Sorry I didn't call, but I've been thinking about you. And I still mean what I told you at the concert."

Linda stood up and put her arm on Shane's shoulder. "Oh, really? Well, there's something I've got to tell you. It's to celebrate your finishing your tape."

Linda reached over with her other hand and picked up one of the full pitchers of soda. Then she stepped away from him. "I wish this were champagne, but it'll have to do," she said. Then she poured the soda over Shane's head. It flattened his hair and soaked his clothes, collecting in puddles on the sawdust-covered floor. Everyone at the table gasped. Then Amy let out a giggle. Pretty soon everyone started laughing. The entire club rang with laughter.

Shane just stood there, soaking wet, saying nothing. Linda put the pitcher back on the table. "I hope everything works out well for you, Shane. But do me a favor—do it without me." She turned to the others. "I'll see you guys later. I have to go up the street and see a *real* show."

She picked up her purse and turned to leave. At the door she saw Kristen. She smiled at Linda and clapped her hands—lightly at first, then harder. Linda smiled back, then hugged Kristen.

She made her way out of Pat's and headed up the street to The Bleecker Café. When she got there she sat down at a table right in front of the stage. Tom's show had just begun.

He was singing when he saw Linda come in. He smiled at her from the stage as he sang the band's opening song. *It's so much more polished than it was the first time I heard it,* Linda thought. And Tom seemed so much more confident and in control of the stage.

When the song was over, Tom looked at Linda. Then he leaned toward the microphone. "We don't normally do a ballad this early in the set, but there's a special reason for us to do this song tonight."

He turned to the band and told them which

one he wanted to play. Then he stepped up to the microphone and began to sing. His voice was as sweet and clear as she had remembered. Only this time, he was singing to her.

Linda's heart rose in her throat. She was so happy she thought she'd burst. And seeing the look in Tom's eyes, she knew how she would finish her painting. She finally knew how it felt to be in love.

We hope you enjoyed reading this book. All the titles currently available in the Sweet Dreams series are listed at the front of the book. They are all available at your local bookshop or newsagent, though should you find any difficulty in obtaining the books you would like, you can order direct from the publisher, at the address below. Also, if you would like to know more about the series, or would simply like to tell us what you think of the series, write to:

Kim Prior
Sweet Dreams
Transworld Publishers Ltd.
61–63 Uxbridge Road
Ealing
London W5 5SA

To order books, please list the title(s) you would like, and send together with a cheque or postal order made payable to TRANSWORLD PUBLISHERS LTD. Please allow the cost of the book(s) plus postage and packing charges as follows:

All orders up to a total of £5.00 : 50p
All orders in excess of £5.00 : Free

Please note that payment must be made in pounds sterling; other currencies are unacceptable.

(The above applies to readers in the UK and Republic of Ireland only)

If you live in Australia or New Zealand and would like more information about the series, please write to:

Sally Porter
Sweet Dreams
Transworld Publishers (Aust) Pty
Ltd.
15-23 Helles Avenue
Moorebank
N.S.W. 2170
AUSTRALIA

Kiri Martin
Sweet Dreams
c/o Corgi and Bantam Books
New Zealand
Cnr. Moselle and Waipareira
Avenues
Henderson
Auckland
NEW ZEALAND

On Our Own

This is a brand new SWEET DREAMS mini-series created by bestselling SWEET DREAMS author Janet Quin-Harkin, and starring best friends Jill and Toni, whose exploits delighted readers of TEN BOY SUMMER and THE GREAT BOY CHASE.

Back from their whirlwind tour of Europe, there's lots of excitement in store for Jill and Toni as they set out to discover if there is life after high school.

Ask your bookseller for titles you have missed:

Kelly Blake

TEEN MODEL

One day she's an A student at Franklyn High with a major crush on the boy next door. Then she's discovered by the head of the prestigious FLASH! modelling agency. Almost overnight, Kelly becomes the hottest new face in the modelling world!

Each of the KELLY BLAKE titles features the ongoing characters and events in Kelly's life. While romance is part of that life, these books are more than romances; they deal with the experiences, conflicts, crises and behind-the-scenes details of modelling.

Ask your bookseller for the titles you have missed:

1. DISCOVERED!
2. RISING STAR

Coming soon:

3. HARD TO GET
4. HEADLINERS
5. DOUBLE TROUBLE
6. PARIS NIGHTS

TRUE LOVE! CRUSHES! BREAKUPS! MAKEUPS!

Find out what it's like to be a COUPLE

Ask your bookseller for any titles you have missed:

Coming soon . . .

COUPLES SPECIAL EDITION
SUMMER HEAT!